A Disco for One

A Romance Mystery

Katherine Martino

For my son, Samuel, with love.

PROLOGUE

It was the party to end all parties; unique because she was wearing the pink sequined dress with the feather trim, unique because she felt good in it, embraced in all its garishness and disco glory, not caring one iota what anyone thought as she sashayed and twirled to Abba's "Dancing Queen". Next was Kylie, followed by Pet Shop Boys and, with each new song, she further continued to shed every deeply ingrained inhibition, every self-conscious feeling and deep-seated torment that had, until this moment, held her back from exhibiting her true palette of colours. A rainbow of crescendo, inuendo and gay abandonment. Never had she felt so liberated and isolated both at the same time.

She stopped to pour another drink, not worrying or even sure if she had already had enough. Tonight, her glass would overflow in a cascade of libation and liberation, and nothing was going to stop her now. Except something did. It was hot, too hot. She stumbled and her head began to pound. Had she really had that much to drink? She needed to get upstairs to bed. Thank goodness she was at home and didn't have far to go. She hoped her bed wasn't covered with coats. Then she remembered, it was also the party to end all parties because it was a party of one. She removed the dress and left it discarded on the floor; like its wearer, it was now a crumpled and lacklustre heap.

Her head had only just touched the pillow when she thought she heard a noise downstairs. Had she really been alone? She couldn't remember. Just in case, she got back up and put on her dress. The effort was almost too much, and as she fell back on the bed, her last thought was that something wasn't right and then she was out like the proverbial light.

Abigail finished playing the music from the '70s and '80s that she knew her mother loved. She had heard that familiar music could sometimes bring a person out of a coma. Her mother looked so peaceful, even though she was in intensive care. Perhaps she had heard the songs from her past, had been transported back to a happier time when all things seemed possible. Abigail tried to take comfort from the fact that she might still be able to do something nice for her mother. She looked inside the bag that the nurse had given her; the clothes her mother had been wearing when the ambulance had transported her from home to the hospital, or so she thought. Abigail was still wearing a puzzled expression when the nurse returned to check on them both.

'I think I have the wrong items.'

The nurse checked her notes methodically, 'No, these are the clothes your mum was wearing, or rather the dress. That's it, no underwear, no shoes.'

'But my mum doesn't own a dress like this. She wouldn't be seen dead in it.' Abigail began to sob as she realized how possibly prophetic and insensitive her last remark must seem. 'I'm so sorry. I wasn't thinking. None of this makes any sense.'

It was still hot, much too hot, but this definitely wasn't her bed; too firm, too institutional. Joanna hadn't wanted the music to stop. She thought she heard a woman's voice. It reminded her of her daughter, Abigail. No! Abigail wouldn't be heard anywhere near the music of her mother's youth. Was her mind playing tricks or was the woman now crying? Crying at her party, that wouldn't do! She tried to open her eyes, nothing happened, she was still enveloped in darkness. She tried to move her arms, signal she was here, but nothing worked. She felt trapped; her spirit, just like her body, crushed.

CHAPTER ONE

"If music be the food of love, play on" – William Shakespeare

Oh, these "what ifs?" The threads, knots and loose ends that hold together the pattern of our lives. They choose to bind, fray or unravel at any given moment. We can either be hemmed in or come apart at the seams. The choice is ours; we are each a seamstress or tailor. Choice, the accomplice and enemy of the "what ifs?", closely rivalled by the "if onlys", but is there always something left to selvedge? What if Phil Collins had never written "One More Night"? If only Joanna had waited until she was sure of Sam before she told Mark that she no longer wanted to continue on in their marriage.

Joanna had met Mark on her 25th birthday, already, and perhaps prematurely, at an age when her heart was beyond broken from believing she could change the bad boys to whom she was inexcusably attracted time and time again. Mark wasn't a bad boy; he was dependable, (she refused to stoop so low as to call him boring). She was sure that he loved her more than she loved him, and here was the problem and why she ended the relationship, albeit with some reluctance. Although not always easy, Joanna tried to behave selflessly. However, it was this element of reluctance, coupled with the grand romantic gesture, that forever changed her destiny.

The grand romantic gesture was delivered in a crude manila envelope, in person, and left in her mailbox. Once retrieved, Joanna immediately recognized her name written in Mark's careful but tiny script. His handwriting mirrored the way he lived, unobtrusive and not wanting to take up more than his fair share of space. It was this trait that made the grand romantic gesture even more grand, for the contents of the envelope revealed more of Mark's miniscule handwriting in the form of the entire lyrics to "One More Night", a popular song of the day by Phil Collins. Joanna didn't much care for the song, even back then she preferred disco and pop, but the grand romantic gesture, as intended, swept her high off her feet and her head remained in the clouds a minute too long. When she fell back to earth, landing at a crossroads, the wide, open road that had lay ahead with all of its delicious twists and turns had become an unpredictable and crazy paved path. Joanna lost her footing and made a wrong turn. She took Mark back.

When it became apparent that things were getting serious, her friends had tried to talk her out of it.

Alison was especially blunt, 'But you're going to have to sleep with him.'

'Okay, I admit he doesn't make my heart go boom, boom, boom, but perhaps the bad boys are just for fun, not to marry. I know Mark loves me and would never do anything to hurt me.'

'But shouldn't marriage also be fun?' Alison softened her tone, 'Joanna, do you honestly love him?'

'Of course I do,' she replied rather too quickly. 'It's a different kind of love.'

'And devoid of all passion.' Alison wasn't trying to be cruel; she was concerned for her friend.

'But he wrote out all the lyrics to "One More Night". That so romantic.'

'And on the strength of that alone, you're going to marry him?'

And that's exactly what Joanna did.

Their marriage had got off to a promising start. Mark was a devoted husband and Joanna enjoyed his companionship at the end of a tiring day. It was nice to find him waiting for her at the station, and to often pick up a carryout meal on the drive home. He was also an excellent cook, and there was nothing she anticipated more than enjoying one of his home cooked meals with a glass of wine while they both talked about their day. It was nice to share the responsibilities of life.

When Joanna became pregnant with Abigail, she happily agreed to be a stay-at-home mum. She had not gone to college, or carved out a career, and happily worked as an admin assistant in order to pay her way. She worked to live, not the other way around. Her life was comfortable and predictable, (she refused to stoop so low as to call it boring). At the beginning, Mark was a doting father. Who wouldn't be? Abigail was a joy, but after a few months, especially when she began to teethe, Joanna found herself wondering if Mark could be jealous of their tiny helpless daughter? She would catch him watching her cuddle and comfort their distressed child, who was red faced and chewing on anything within her grasp, with a look that bordered on resentment. Once her mind started to wander down this road, Joanna found she couldn't stop. She had always told herself that every marriage was different, requiring components unique to the specific individuals to work, and that everyone had their own expectations and definitions of love. But had she been trying to delude herself in order to not pass blame? Of course, there was no-one else to blame but herself. She had realized early on that she didn't love Mark in the way he loved her, but she had worked hard to not let it show. Was she now guilty of letting her guard down? She appreciated Mark, had done everything to be considerate of his feelings, but was that enough to sustain their relationship in the years to come and ensure they grew old together? And now, with the addition of this precious baby, was the chasm too great to be inconspicuous? The seed, now sown, took root and slowly flourished until it strangled like ivy. Not only for the sake of their daughter but because they genuinely cared for one another, Mark and Joanna tried several times to get their now obvious derailed relationship back on track.

Whenever they were going through an especially rough patch, Mark would arrange to cook something special for just the two of them. Joanna knew that this signalled that he wanted to talk. Dinner would begin with them eating in silence, then making small talk until Mark felt the time was right to tell her how he felt and how he thought she was feeling too. He always began in the same way. He would put down his fork in a deliberate manner that wasn't meant to appear deliberate, take a sip of wine and then look her in the eye.

'Have I done something to make you unhappy?'

He would apportion the blame to himself, which always irritated her, and she would counter with, 'No, you haven't done anything.'

'Then why do I get the sense that something's wrong?'

'Mark, it isn't anything you've done. I guess we're at that point in our marriage when neither one of us knows how to make the other happy.'

'But I'm not unhappy in our marriage. Are you?'

She should have answered yes, but what would be the point when there was nothing he could do to make things right? The problem was hers alone and she would just have to live with it.

'No, I'm fine. I guess what I meant to say is that when you've been married as long as us, things can get a little stale.'

'So, what can I do to fix it?'

There he went again, bearing all the responsibility.

'We're fine. Nothing needs to be fixed.'

'Are you sure? I love you, Joanna.'

'And I love you too.'

This was always the cue for them to go upstairs and have sex. Afterwards, Joanna would lie awake remembering the bad boys who had made her heart go boom, boom, boom. Had they, too, finally settled into stale marriages or were they now even more adept in the art of keeping passion alive? Some nights her mind would wander even further and she would find herself reliving some of those moments of passion with the bad boys. She'd recall the small but important details that made them all so irresistible: Ricky's long eyelashes, the way Nick's hair curled at the nape of his neck and over his collar. Details that were not lost on the countless other women they charmed, for trust and loyalty were never on their list of attributes. The memories of unbridled passion were not the only reason she felt hot, she also was blushing from one especially embarrassing recollection. One evening, Nick found himself working late and alone at the office and called Joanna to ask if she fancied keeping him company. They had been unable to keep their hands off one another and had ended up making love on the office floor. Unfortunately, locking the door was not enough to keep out prying eyes. The building was located on a busy city street and Nick's office just happened to be at the same level as the upper deck of a sightseeing bus that was stopped at a light, full of tourists. With floor to ceiling windows and no blinds, Joanna happened to turn her head and realised they had an audience. A sea of bemused faces greeted her. Yes, as hard as it now seemed, she continued to hold on to the conviction that she had done the right thing by marrying Mark, if only to preserve her dignity.

Neither Mark nor Joanna had entered into their marriage with the idea that if it didn't work there was the option of divorce. It continued to limp along, and there were times when there were glimmers of hope, but by the time Abigail had finished college and begun living her own life, the end was only a matter of time. Looking back now, Joanna was glaringly aware that when she had said her marriage vows she had bet everything on the "better" and lost. The final year was spent living separate lives.

One evening, and as a last minute decision, Joanna went alone to see Kylie Minogue perform at a downtown venue, and that was when and where she found herself sitting next to Sam. Her seat should have been occupied by Sam's housemate, Mickey, but Mickey had cancelled at the last minute. Sam told her that Mickey was a fashion designer, with a show coming up, and he had to stay behind to make some last minute alterations and finishing touches to his collection. His pièce de résistance was a Kylie inspired dress which Mickey thought that, other than the songstress herself, he could wear better than any model on the catwalk. Joanna immediately found herself laughing and warming to Sam. She was glad she had found the confidence to venture out alone and she discovered that she was enjoying herself far more than if Mark had been there with her. By the end of the evening, she knew that Sam was a Professor at the local college, teaching a course on the History of European Pop Music, and he had invited her to Mickey's fashion show which was also taking place at the college. She could barely contain her excitement, nor hide her new found lease on life from Mark. She felt deceitful, disloyal and guilty.

A week before the fashion show it all became too much to bear and she asked Mark for a divorce. She hadn't expected him to look so hurt and crushed, nor been prepared for the wave of emotion that threatened to drown her resolve. She had heard people liken the end of a marriage to a bereavement and, even though the decision had been at her instigation, she was taken aback by the enormity of her own feeling of grief. She had naively expected to only feel relief and had counted on Mark to also feel the same way.

'Is there someone else?' Mark asked, almost inaudibly.

His directness unnerved her, but he had every right to know. 'There's no easy way to say this but, yes, I've recently met someone who I want to spend more time with. I would never sneak around and go behind your back, which is why I'm telling you now before the inevitable happens.' In Joanna's mind anything less would have been adultery.

Surely the end of their marriage was inevitable? They had let it continue far too long past its best by date. This was more complicated than she had first thought. It wasn't that she now doubted her decision but that she was ill prepared for the sadness that accompanied it and threatened to overwhelm and obliterate her initial feeling of relief.

The following weekend they did their best to explain their decision to their daughter, as maturely and respectfully as their feelings would permit.

'But I thought you both loved one another. That's what you always told me.'

'And we still do and always will.' Mark tried to unsuccessfully offer words of comfort.

'Then why are you getting a divorce?'

Abigail began to cry uncontrollably, and neither Joanna nor Mark could suppress their own tears. As the three of them witnessed firsthand, when it came to divorce, they were all children with hard to rein in emotions that felt new and raw. They all sat on the sofa, arms around each other, holding one another so tightly that each could hardly muster the breath to sob.

That Sunday evening, after Abigail had left, Mark stood in the hallway with his suitcase.

'If you need to get in touch, I'll be staying with Eloise.'

Joanna tried not to look surprised. Eloise was his former high school sweetheart. They had briefly been engaged. So, he had had someone waiting in the wings all along. He gave her a chaste hug and left.

Joanna was excited. Excited and surprised. She hadn't been sure how she would feel when the day of the fashion show arrived. Given all that had gone before, she wasn't sure if she would even be able to muster up enough enthusiasm to go, but here she was dancing around her bedroom as she threw numerous possible outfit combinations onto her bed. As well as details for the show, Sam had also sent her two Italian disco songs. He and Mickey had spent some time in Rome and Milan. She loved that in just one short meeting he had already expanded her musical repertoire. She couldn't understand one word of the lyrics, but she already loved them anyway. She picked up a vibrant silk dress. She was unsure. She didn't want to over-egg the pudding; Joanna being the pudding and the array of clothes the eggs. She decided to save the silk dress for a future date, (was she getting ahead of herself, being too optimistic?), finally opting for black pants, black silk top and a dusty pink long jacket with a waterfall collar that had always garnered her compliments. Not too flamboyant but not too understated either. She accessorized with a vintage Bakelite bracelet, pink with raised flowers. She twirled in front of the mirror and, for the first time in probably years, felt genuinely happy. She positively glowed.

Although she arrived early, the auditorium was already full and buzzing with excitement and enthusiasm. The student fashion show was an annual event and always culminated with the showing of a collection by its former star pupil, Mickey Harman. It was one of the highlights of the academic year with all the proceeds from sponsors and ticket sales going to a charity voted for by the students. Well attended by the local and national press, it was great publicity for all involved and had launched many a career, including Mickey's. Joanna gave her name at the door and was warmly greeted by one of Sam's students.

'Hello, Professor McLaughlin asked me to take good care of you. Please follow me to your seat.'

She made Sam sound very important, and Joanna too, by association. She found herself sitting in the front row.

'Professor McLaughlin is still backstage, putting the finishing touches to the music. He asked me to tell you that he will be out shortly.'

Joanna had only just sat down when she glimpsed the back of Sam's tall frame. He was dressed in white jeans and a vibrant blue sleeveless hoodie over a lime green t shirt which perfectly suited his sandy coloured hair. She didn't have to wait long for him to come over and take his seat next to her.

'I'm so pleased you could make it.'

The colour of his shirt made his eyes appear even bluer. Joanna caught her breath, 'I wouldn't have missed this for the world. Thank you for inviting me.'

Sam smiled, 'You're going to love the music. I chose it myself.'

Before she had a chance to reply, the first of the models, all students at the college, came walking down the runway. Joanna was impressed, not only by the designs, but their professionalism. They would not have looked out of place on the runways of Paris or Milan. There were three collections and then it was Mickey's turn. The first dress was greeted with loud cheers and applause. It was comprised of a cream leotard top and white feather skirt. The model, who had the grace and posture of a ballerina, suited it perfectly as she pirouetted and danced down the runway to the gentle rock sound of Marc Bolan singing "Ride a White Swan". Joanna could hardly restrain herself from jumping up and dancing on the runway with her. She loved the music of Marc Bolan. Each garment that followed was just as exquisite and so was the soundtrack. Just when she thought it couldn't get any more perfect, she heard the first strains and hypnotic pulsating beat of "If I Can't Dance" by Sophie Ellis-Bextor, and Mickey appeared wearing his pièce de résistance, the dress for which he had missed seeing Kylie. Barefoot, he flounced along the runway in pink sequins and feather trim. He reminded Joanna of Marc Bolan, the same diminutive stature and dark corkscrew hair; Lord Byron on steroids. When he was parallel to them, Mickey turned to Sam and shot him a cheeky grin. When his piercing green eyes fell on Joanna, his look was one of ice but, so brief, she couldn't be entirely sure. She hoped she was wrong. Mickey turned, shook his Marc Bolan curls, and skipped back to the start of the runway where he was enveloped by his models. They all danced and twirled their way back to the audience, accompanied by the '80s synth sound of the Pet Shop Boys' "What Have I Done to Deserve This?", and were greeted with a standing ovation. After the music stopped and the lights had dimmed, Sam asked her if she had enjoyed herself.

'Everything was wonderful, and you were right about the music, I love Marc Bolan. His was the first concert I ever went to, the Dandy in the Underworld tour.'

Sam looked genuinely impressed, 'Wow, I'd love to hear your memories of that time. I teach a separate course on the origins of Glam Rock. Listen, let's meet for a drink one evening after work next week. I need to go backstage now and help Mickey. I'd introduce you, but now's not a good time. He can be a little temperamental right after a show, a lot of analysing and self-criticism about what could've gone better. Once he's done the press interviews, and everyone has confirmed that he's awesome, he settles down. I hope you understand.'

'Of course I do.'

Secretly, Joanna was relieved not to have to meet Mickey face to face after the look he had given her. Perhaps it was all down to the stress of the evening.

'I'll look forward to us getting together next week.'

'I'll be in touch.'

Sam made his way backstage and Joanna headed for her car. She listened to Marc Bolan as she drove, and by the time she was home, all she could think about was how fantastic the evening had been and that she couldn't wait to see Sam again.

CHAPTER TWO

Sam was ten years older than Mickey, but he could sometimes be quite childlike. Mickey could act wiser than his years. They made an ideal couple, but Mickey had his demons.

Mickey's life changed forever on his tenth birthday. He raced home from school in eager anticipation of presents and cake. He was not disappointed. His parents had got him an artist's set; a beautiful monogrammed rosewood box full of assorted chalks, paints, pens and pencils in every colour imaginable. After dinner, and after he had blown out the candles on his cake and made a wish, he was given the news. If he had known what was about to be imparted, he would have wished for something else. At first, he thought his parents were about to tell him they were getting a divorce. In retrospect, he would have preferred it. So many of his friends now spent alternate weekends with one parent or the other, and with new and sometimes improved families, that he often felt the odd one out. But this knowledge left him feeling even more isolated, together with a loss of identity. He wondered how many times his parents had rehearsed this conversation. It seemed so scripted until his mother became very emotional.

'No-one could convince me that I didn't go to the hospital and give birth to you myself.'

Was this supposed to make him feel better? 'Why didn't my mum want to keep me?' The question had to be asked, although Mickey was afraid of the answer.

His mum was crying now, 'I'm sure she did, honey, but she was still a child herself. There wasn't any way she could have taken care of you.'

'What about my dad?'

'I think he was also very young.'

'How old was I when you adopted me?'

'Six months.' Mickey's dad was speaking now. 'Each time your mum got pregnant, she miscarried, so we decided to adopt. You were the answer to our prayers.'

That evening, and alone in his room, Mickey took out his new pencils and began to sketch what would eventually become the basis of his portfolio. He drew numerous images of a woman, how he imagined his mother, wearing glamourous gowns and always holding the hand of a child. Fashion design was a natural progression and afforded him the tools to quell and manage his emotions. It gave him the power to make women admire and need him, to look and behave with his approval, even if only for the duration of a fitting or a show. He used his creativity as a way to continuously strive to make amends for what he perceived to be his mother's decision to abandon him. He was continually driven to make her proud. His creations afforded him control and sometimes they controlled him. From that moment on no-one could ever love him enough; only Sam came close.

Mickey had wanted to dislike Joanna on sight, but when he saw her, albeit briefly, seated next to Sam in the front row, his instant impression was of someone personable and kind, not of a desperate older woman trying too hard. Nevertheless, he was relieved to see Sam enter the backstage area alone. He had hoped that Sam would be sensitive to his mood, to know not to bring Joanna, but he hadn't been sure. He couldn't be sure about anything when it came to this new friend, and here was the problem. From the moment Sam had returned home from the Kylie concert, something seemed different. Of course he was elated, that was to be expected, who wouldn't be after seeing Kylie? No, something had happened, and that something was meeting Joanna. Sam didn't mention her immediately, but when he did, it was obvious that she had made an impression and he wanted to see her again, so it came as no surprise when he said he had invited her to the fashion show. Sam had numerous women friends, and one or two were close confidantes, but never before had Mickey felt threatened by them. Yes, that was exactly how he felt. In their one short meeting, he believed that Joanna was already on the way to owning a piece of Sam's heart. The perceived threat had now grown infinitely greater, and Mickey was already setting it up to implode. Mickey also knew

13

that Sam loved him and would never intentionally hurt him, and that he hadn't even realised the effect Joanna had had; otherwise listening to Sam go on about their shared easygoing conversation and 'wasn't it a stroke of luck that she had bought his ticket at the last minute' would have been deliberately hurtful and cruel. Sam wasn't even thinking of Joanna in that way. Had Mickey asked, he would have said that he was a gay man who had enjoyed an evening in the company of a woman. Nothing more, nothing less.

As Sam had anticipated, Mickey was sitting alone in a corner, full of self-doubt. He was still wearing his Kylie dress. Sam gave him a hug and a kiss, blissfully unaware of the thoughts and emotions tearing through the very fibre of Mickey's soul.

'You and your collection were awesome, as always. It was a bloody brilliant evening but I know you won't just take my word for it.'

Mickey gave him a weak smile. Just at that moment, one of the students came to tell him that the press was assembled and waiting.

His mood changed instantly as he jumped down from the stool, ran his fingers through his hair, tilted his head and, with an impish grin, announced to the whole world, 'I'm ready for my close up!'

The room was full of reporters and flashing cameras. Mickey recognised familiar faces from both local and national press, together with those from the trade papers. Charisma oozed from his every pore, and the minute he entered the room, he owned it and knew. His designs spoke for themselves, but he was the perfect ambassador for his creations. The media adored him. Even though he took himself very seriously, he never let on, and always presented himself as lighthearted and full of humour.

'Please tell us the inspiration for the pink dress which, I might add, you wear beautifully,' was the first question.

'I designed this entire collection with both Kylie and Sophie Ellis-Bextor in mind but, you're right, I do wear it rather well. I want everyone to be able to wear my clothes. I design for the world.'

'And why did you choose these two particular artists?'

'Because, as well as being super talented, they are glamourous, fun and real, just like my clothes. We can all relate to them in some part. My designs can be worn on stage but don't look out of place at the clubs and restaurants. I want everyone to be able to feel good about themselves. My motivation is to always work towards building confidence in the wearer.'

14

Sam watched from the doorway. Mickey sure knew how to work a crowd. When the press conference was over, he exhibited none of the self-doubt and angst that had plagued him earlier. He had received his seal of approval, for now. His mother would be proud.

They drove home in silence until Sam asked Mickey if he had noticed Joanna seated next to him at the show.

'Yes, I did. At first glance she looked older than I imagined, given her taste in music.'

Mickey felt sure that Sam jumped to Joanna's defence when he replied, 'She's amazing, a breath of fresh air, not at all what you'd expect. Do you know she likes Marc Bolan? Even went to one of his concerts.'

'Then she is old.' Mickey regretted his words, the minute they were out, but he couldn't help himself.

Sam continued as though he hadn't heard. 'I'm meeting her for a drink next week to hear her memories of Marc. Do you still have that vintage button with the pearlised swan on it, the one you found at the estate sale in Italy?'

'Yes, I do. Try as I might, there isn't much I can do with just the one button. I always hoped I would find a use for it.' Mickey thought he knew where Sam was going with this line of questioning but hoped he was wrong.

'Would you mind if I gave it to Joanna? You know, the Marc Bolan, Ride a White Swan connection. I think she'd appreciate it.'

'Of course, I don't mind,' Mickey lied.

His hunch had been right and, unlike the swan, his feathers were ruffled.

Sam was already waiting when Joanna arrived at the tapas bar; situated close to the college, it seemed an ideal place to meet. She was wearing her vibrant silk dress. Sam got up from the table to greet her. He offered his hand but she had already reached out for a hug. He was caught a little off guard, unsure whether it was a result of her show of affection or that she looked breathtakingly beautiful.

'Joanna, you look absolutely stunning.' The words escaped before he could draw on some kind of restraint. He wanted to grab them, pull them back and hide them in his pocket, especially when he saw her look of delight; a look that conveyed more than her pleasure at receiving the compliment. It was an expression of optimism. For a moment he hesitated about giving her the swan button. He realised how easy it would be to also give her the wrong impression. Joanna was oblivious to his faux pas. She had been looking forward to this evening all week. She was continually amazed at how happy and optimistic she felt these days. Even her co-workers had noticed this new buoyancy and were impressed by her ability to bounce back so quickly from the demise of her marriage. Sam ordered them each a glass of Prosecco, then reached into his pocket and brought out the button.

'Here, I have something to give you. Mickey found this at an estate sale in Italy. I know how much you like "Ride a White Swan". It can be your lucky talisman.'

Joanna held the green Bakelite button and ran her finger over the raised pearlised swan motif. She couldn't remember ever being given anything so perfect, certainly not by Mark. How could this man, who she had known for such a short time, read her so perfectly?

'Oh Sam, thank you! It's exquisite, I'll treasure it forever.'

Sam was happy to have chosen to give the button to Joanna, but he couldn't shake a nagging doubt that she might have already read too much into the gesture.

Over tapas, Joanna enthused about the fashion show and Mickey's designs, especially the pink sequined dress.

'Yes, Mickey is very talented. You must meet him. Why don't you come over for dinner one evening? I'll cook us all an authentic Italian meal.' It would then be obvious to her that he and Mickey were a couple, 'but right now, I want to hear all about when you went to see Marc Bolan in concert.'

Joanna warmed to her subject, 'It was his last ever tour in 1977. I had always loved his music, but my parents said I was too young to go to a concert until Dandy in the Underworld. Marc gave a fantastic performance. The fans were still screaming, just like they had done at his Wembley concerts five years earlier.'

'Yes, it's both tragic and ironic that he was killed in a car crash at a time when he was starting to enjoy a resurgence in both his career and popularity, and only two weeks before his thirtieth birthday.'

'His death had such an effect on me that I went to his funeral. I stood outside with all the other fans. I remember talking to a woman, she must only have been about twenty years old. She told me that she worked as Marc's receptionist in his management office. She'd got the job after standing outside his office with other fans. She'd got to know the people who worked there, and when they needed a receptionist, they offered her the position. She told me that even though she could have gone inside for the funeral, she chose to stand outside with the fans, because first and foremost she would always be one of them and it was where she belonged. It just shows the power of music. It inspires you to feel and do so much. It can totally transform your life. It did hers.'

Perhaps it was the Prosecco, or perhaps it was just Joanna's way, but Sam had never heard his exact feelings on music expressed so eloquently and from the heart. Despite all the internal warnings, he reached across the table and squeezed her hand. They sat like that for just a moment too long. Sam wasn't sure what was happening, but Joanna was certain that she had found her soulmate.

At the end of the evening, Sam asked if he could use Joanna's Marc Bolan story in one of his lessons on Glam Rock. She eagerly agreed.

'Of course, and if I think of anything else, I'll let you know over that delicious Italian meal you are going to cook.'

Damn, he'd forgotten all about that. Right now, it didn't seem like a very good idea, but he couldn't withdraw the invitation. Instead, he said, 'I look forward to it. I'll check with Mickey and get back to you with a date.'

Yes, Mickey, why did he feel disloyal? Everything would come right when Joanna saw them both together; he would make sure of it. Joanna moved forward to hug him goodnight, but Sam pretended to be searching for his car keys.

'I must have left them inside on the table,' he lied, 'you go on ahead. I'll be in touch.'

If Joanna was disappointed, she didn't show it. The evening had been perfect. When she was in her car, she looked again at the swan button. Her good luck charm was already working its magic.

Sam arrived home to find Mickey on the sofa, watching "Project Runway". He had his sketch book on his lap.

'Stealing other people's designs again, I see.' Sam's attempt at a lighthearted comment failed miserably. Mickey didn't even acknowledge Sam's presence, least of all his dismal attempt at a joke. Sam walked over to the sofa, knelt down in front of Mickey and took both his hands in his, 'I missed you.'

'Why? You only saw me this morning.'

'Yes, but it's gone eleven. I've been gone the entire day.' Sam hoped he wasn't coming across as trying too hard.

'So, how was your evening with JOAnNAh?' Mickey emphasised each vowel of her name.

Sam pretended not to notice. 'We had a very nice evening. She had some great stories about Marc Bolan. I am going to use them in my syllabus on Glam Rock. She loved the button, by the way.' Mickey was silent, so Sam continued, 'I've invited her here for dinner. I'll cook something Italian. Think about what you would like.'

'Are you sure you wouldn't prefer that I made myself scarce for the evening?' This time Mickey stared straight at him, not even blinking.

'Mickey! If I didn't know you better, no, correction, if I didn't know us better, I'd think you were jealous.'

Mickey fired back, 'Does JOAnNAh know that you and I are an "us"?'

Sam sidestepped what felt like a direct and deserved accusation. 'It's not important whether she does or she doesn't. She's just a friend and I hope she'll become our friend. That's why I've invited her over to meet you. Anyway, not that it's of any consequence, but when she sees the two of us together, she'll know our situation.'

But try as he could to believe his own words, Sam inwardly knew that it was of an enormous consequence. He loved Mickey, he wanted to be with Mickey for the rest of his life, but there was something about Joanna that had touched his very soul.

CHAPTER THREE

Abigail let herself into her mother's house using the spare key that she had first been given back in Middle School. This had been her childhood home where she had grown up. She almost tripped over a rustic wooden plaque lying on the floor of the hallway. It must have fallen off the wall. She picked it up and hung it back, remembering how thrilled she had been when she had found it as a gift for her mother's birthday. The inscription was perfect, "I may be old, but that's ok, I got to see Marc Bolan in concert!" She stopped by the living room. She was surprised not to see an empty bottle of Prosecco. Instead, there was an almost empty pitcher with an almost full glass of a blue liquid close by. It looked as though her mother's preference in alcohol had changed recently. The rest of the room and house looked tidy. When she reached Joanna's bedroom, Abigail opened the closet. She was still carrying the pink sequined dress. As she had correctly remembered, there was nothing in Joanna's collection of clothes that reflected this choice. Most were the colourful but tailored suits that she wore to work as a receptionist for a commercial real estate company. When she went out, she always wore something classic and simple, preferring to up the ante with a flamboyant accessory or two. She had an impressive array of scarves, necklaces, bags and shoes, many vintage. Abigail held the dress against this backdrop but she couldn't find where it might fit. Just like her taste in alcohol, had her mother's taste in clothes also changed? She noticed an unusual button with a swan motif lying on the bedside table. She had never seen Joanna wear anything with buttons like that before or she would surely have remembered. She sat down on the bed. She had sat on this bed, next to her mother, when Joanna had first told her about meeting Sam. That was six months ago. The house felt cosy and still like home. It was smaller than the others on the street and also small by current standards. Joanna always referred to it as her cottage. Not a fan of housework, she rated a house in 'vacuuming hours'; her cottage was just the right fit. For the most part, they had been happy here and Abigail hoped there would be more happy years ahead for her mother. She remembered how elated Joanna had been when she had opened up about Sam. She literally sparkled and shone, as though someone had taken some polish and given every inch of her a bloody good rub. Was she only just now noticing how the last few years of marriage had dulled her mother's very being? Joanna said that meeting a man like Sam, who shared so many of her passions, seemed too good to be true which prompted Abigail to ask if he was gay. She immediately regretted voicing this flippant assumption; a fleeting shadow of panic had crossed Joanna's face. Abigail rather too hurriedly added that Sam sounded like a great friend and she was pleased that her mum now had someone to accompany her to concerts and the such. The conversation ended right there and Abigail knew that her mother was hoping for more than companionship. She had wanted more for Joanna, too, and had her fingers crossed that "too good to be true" would translate into a "happy coincidence".

Abigail looked at the time, remembered it was Monday, and realized that she needed to call her mother's place of work to let them know that Joanna wouldn't be in. She soon discovered that she needn't have bothered as they weren't expecting her; Joanna had booked the week off for a vacation. Why hadn't her mother told her? Where had she planned to go?

As she opened the door to leave, she found Joanna's neighbour, Eileen, standing on the doorstep.

'Hello, Abigail. I saw your car and came to ask how your mum's doing.'

'Not good. She's in intensive care. I'm going back to the hospital now. Thank you for calling the ambulance. You probably saved her life.'

'Oh, it wasn't me. I don't know who called them. I came over when I heard the sirens and saw the lights flashing. The paramedics were knocking on the door, so I let them in with the spare key. There was no-one else here with your mum. They asked me if I knew her next of kin, so I gave them your name and number.'

Who had called the ambulance and why didn't they stay, Abigail thought, but to Eileen she said, 'Well, thank you for doing that. I must get back to the hospital. I'll keep you updated.'

What other mysterious life was her mother leading?

On her way back to the hospital, Abigail stopped by her office. It was lunchtime and she was relieved that hardly any of her co-workers were around. She knew they would be concerned about Joanna but she wasn't in the mood for their questions. She immediately found what she needed, a number for Terry, a reporter she knew who worked for the local paper.

'Hi Terry, it's Abigail and I need a favour.'

'Abigail, how nice to hear from you. How are you?'

'In a bit of a pickle and I need your help.'

'Okay, what's the problem?'

'My mum's been rushed to hospital. Someone called an ambulance but I don't know who it was. No-one does. I want to be able to personally thank them because they saved mum's life. Any chance you could ask one of your contacts for an audio copy of the call? I might recognise the voice.'

'I'm sorry about your mum. I have a contact at the emergency service response centre. I'll get in touch and ask for a copy.'

'Thanks so much, Terry. It will help a lot. The call would have come in very early Sunday morning and dispatched to135 Coolgardie.'

'Sure. No problem, and wish your mum better for me.'

'Will do and thanks again.'

At least Terry had found the reason for her request plausible.

She was walking back into the hospital when her phone rang. It was Mark returning a call she'd made earlier.

'Hi dad, I was calling to let you know about mum.'

'Why? Has something happened?'

'Yes, she was rushed to hospital in the early hours of yesterday morning, unconscious.'

'What's wrong?'

'They don't know, they're still doing tests.'

'How bad is she?'

'Pretty bad, I'm the only visitor she's allowed.'

It sounded as though he was holding back tears. Why hadn't she been more sympathetic, told him gently rather than just blurting it out? Perhaps she should have chosen to not tell him over the phone and arranged to meet face to face. Just because they weren't together any longer didn't automatically cancel out a lifetime of being married.

'Dad? Are you okay?'

'This has come as a bit of a shock.'

'I know.'

'Let me know when I can see her but I would rather not bump into the boyfriend.'

'Don't worry, when she's allowed visitors, you'll be the first to see her.'

'Thanks, Abbey, I do still care about your mum. Always will.'

'Of course.'

She wished she could do something so that her parents would get back together, but she'd already meddled once, in Joanna's relationship with Sam. She would put it on the backburner. She needed her mum to get better first.

* * * * *

Sleep was overrated and she had slept too long. The proof was that her head still hurt and she hoped her hangover would soon be gone; it did feel as though some of the pain had dissipated. What on earth, and how much, had she drunk to make her feel this way? She must get up and begin to tidy the place. Judging by how she felt, it must be a real mess. Very slowly, she eased herself a little. The bed still felt different, and as her dress brushed her skin, she became aware that it no longer felt like flamboyant, pink sequined material but more ill-fitting and functional. It reminded her of a hospital gown. She strained to open her eyes. It took effort and enormous strength, but when achieved, she rushed to close them again; the light was too bright. Had she left the lights on all night? And there was that voice again. It WAS the voice of her daughter. She heard clearly Abigail calling, 'Mum! Mum!' over and over again.

'It's alright, Abigail. I'm here. What's wrong?' Joanna sought to comfort her overwrought daughter. But her words were inaudible. Had she even said them? She couldn't feel her lips move but she was aware that her eyes, behind still closed lids, were moving vigorously.

'Nurse, nurse, my mum just opened her eyes!' Abigail's voice again but why was she addressing a nurse? And now Joanna heard the music again, the music of her youth and the music that she continued to love. Had she also left the music streaming all night? She hoped she hadn't woken the neighbours. She must check and, if necessary, apologise. This was all too much; she must get out of bed and get going. Put her world and Abigail's to rights. It took several attempts but she finally fought the blinding light and kept her eyes open. She couldn't move her head and stared at the light too long. She had spots in front of her eyes, and when she became aware of Abigail leaning over her, the spots were all over Abigail's face and reminded her of the time her daughter was five years old and had caught the measles. Joanna smiled at the memory. At least she thought she did because none of her facial muscles worked. They felt encased in plastic, as if shrink wrapped. Now a strange, but kindly woman, was leaning over her, speaking to her, softly and reassuringly, as she poked and prodded and did all manner of things. Joanna thought she heard Abigail crying but she had moved out of view to make way for the kindly woman. What on earth had happened and where was she? Joanna tried to ask but it seemed as though only her eyes moved and blinked in a kind of morse code. Just as she felt she must make contact, all fight left her, her weary eyes closed and a peaceful darkness engulfed her. In the midst of this blackness, she thought she heard Abigail speak. She thought she heard her ask the kindly woman if this was a good sign. She was sure she heard the kindly woman reply that it was too soon to tell, that she must not become agitated and this was why she must be sedated. Sedated? Who had been sedated? Where was she? What was going on? Joanna needed answers. She needed to be there for Abigail, reassure her as she had always done, but it was all too much. The darkness engulfed her, sapped her of all energy. She fell back into a drug induced sleep to the strains of Abba singing "The Winner Takes It All".

* * * * *

Abigail sat by her mother's bedside all night. She kept the music playing softly in the hope that it might elicit a response, a second awakening. What had happened to her mother the night of the supposed party? Had she really been alone? Why was there so much interest in the toxicology report? As crazy as it seemed, Abigail believed that the pink sequined dress held a major clue. With all these questions whirring in her head like a disco ball, as dawn approached, she too fell into a deep sleep. When she awoke, there was an email from Terry with an attachment. It was the audio of the ambulance call. Abigail played it through four times to be absolutely certain that she didn't recognise the voice. If she had known the person, she would have been able to place him immediately because of the unusual way he enunciated her mother's name. Who had called the ambulance that night? Had he been with her throughout and harmed her, or found her and called for help? Her phone beeped again, this time it was a text from Sam.

Hi Abigail, sorry to bother you but I have been trying to reach your mum. Do you know where she is? Is there something up with her phone?

Sam! Of course! He would probably know about the vacation, and he might be able to shed some light on the dress.

Abigail had only met Sam once. It was a few days after Joanna had been to the tapas bar. Her mum had called her to tell her all about it. Abigail sensed correctly that Joanna was at her most fragile and vulnerable and had probably been so for some time. She also felt remorse at not having noticed this in her mother sooner. Abigail was sure that Joanna was placing all of her eggs in one basket and, in order to be of help, Abigail was required to walk on every one of these eggshells. In order to avert an emotional disaster, it was necessary to meet Sam and make sure her mother wasn't reading too much into things. It would be easy to get Sam's email address at the college but what reason could she use for wanting to meet up with him alone? She eventually came up with the excuse of being interested in taking a course at the college but not wanting her mother to know because it would worry her if she thought Abigail was unhappy and thinking of switching careers. She thought it might sound rather lame but Sam must have bought it because he replied almost immediately and they arranged to meet at a restaurant close to Abigail's office. They both arrived at the same time and she instantly knew why Joanna was smitten. As well as having the bluest eyes she'd ever seen, his relaxed ambience would immediately put even the most uptight of individuals at ease. Abigail was sure that the classes he taught were the most popular at the school with, probably, a mile long wait list. The restaurant was busy and they had to wait to give their order. Abigail put down her menu.

'I'm usually quite impatient, not a good trait in a paralegal, but I'm pleased our food is taking a long time as I want to know everything about you.'

'I'm really quite boring. You'll know everything there is to know before you've finished your appetizer.'

'That's not what my mum said. She thinks you're really interesting. Meeting you is the best thing that's happened to her in years.' Abigail was surprised at her directness.

'I think Joanna's very interesting, too. Not at all what I expected.'

'She said you've been a professor at the local college for several years.'

'Yes, I teach a course on the History of European Pop Music.'

'Ah, that explains a lot. Mum loves pop, disco and Eurovision but I expect she's already told you that.'

'Yes. It's great to actually meet someone who grew up listening to the music and you must have heard the songs as lullabies.'

'Absolutely. I was a disco dancing, sleep deprived baby. But, on a more serious note, I'm so pleased that my mum's met someone who shares her passion for all things pop. Dad preferred Genesis and Pink Floyd, probably why they're now getting a divorce.'

'I'm sorry, I hope there's more to it than that. Relationships require a lot of effort.'

'Sounds as though you're speaking from experience.'

'By the time you reach 47, you've been around the block a few times.'

'Ever been married, Sam?'

'No.'

'Ever come close?'

'Not in the traditional sense.'

'Intriguing answer.'

'Is that the concerned daughter or the paralegal talking?'

'Both. I'm not entirely sure I get your meaning.'

'Love is love. It comes in many forms, but there's still not enough of it to go around, which is why you have to hold on tight when you find it.'

'Profound. I appreciate there's a slight age difference but do you think you might find it with mum?'

'Abigail, we're friends who share the same taste in music.'

'Do you already have a girlfriend?'

'No.'

'Why not?' She couldn't refrain from asking the question. This was so unlike her.

'I'm not looking for one.'

'I bet some of your students have huge crushes on you.'

'I'd never jeopardise my career.'

'Ah, so there have been some crushes.'

'You're a paralegal with a vivid imagination. That's enough about me. You've finished your appetizer, so let's talk about something else.'

'Not yet. I want to convince you to date my mother.' She was embarrassed for Joanna at how desperate she must sound.

'Abigail, you're making this very awkward. I'm sure your mum would be mortified if she knew we were having this conversation. She doesn't know, does she?'

'Of course she doesn't know.'

'That's a relief. I was beginning to wonder if she might have put you up to this.'

'No, not at all.'

'Let's change the subject before I lose my appetite.'

'I think you're hiding something.'

'As I've already said, you've got a vivid imagination.'

'Alright, I'll drop it for now, but I think you'd be perfect for one another.'

'Your mum's a fascinating woman.'

'Then it's your loss and you're making no sense.'

There was an awkward pause in the conversation, and even though Abigail tried her hardest to take a lighter stance throughout the rest of the meal, and chat more about the courses offered by the college, the damage had already been done. She hoped she hadn't ruined things for her mother. She had left the restaurant concerned that she might be left to pick up a lot of pieces of eggshell. For his part, Sam was surprised at how defensive he felt and hoped that when he next saw Joanna, whatever these feelings were, would all come out in the wash.

CHAPTER FOUR

Sam didn't immediately set a date for the dinner. He toyed with the idea of cancelling the evening altogether, but there was a part of him that wanted to see Joanna again, and with Mickey present. He wanted to prove to himself, just as much as to Mickey, that all he and Joanna shared was a camaraderie borne out of them having the same taste in music.

It was Mickey who unwittingly came to the rescue, making the decision for him by letting Sam know that he had a craving for Eggplant Parmigiana, followed by Tiramisu for dessert.

'Are you sure you wouldn't like me to make it for just the two of us?' Sam asked.

Mickey was taken aback and rather pleased by this change of heart, but he didn't let on, instead replying, 'No, go ahead and invite JOAnNAh. If it's just the two of us, I'll end up eating her portion as well and won't be able to fit into my fabulous creations.'

If Sam was surprised by Mickey's new found ambience, he didn't let it show. He had no intention of jeopardising his relationship with Mickey any further.

Joanna was experiencing a quandary of her own. As each day passed with no invitation from Sam, she became more anxious to the point where she found herself retracing her steps, trying to determine where she might have put a foot wrong, perhaps overstepped the mark at their previous get together at the tapas bar. When she did eventually get a text, the relief was so great, she burst into tears. She tried to compose herself but went into a tailspin wondering what to wear and what kind of wine to take. She couldn't shake off the hunch that Mickey would waste no time in throwing her under the microscope, as well as probably a bus!

Joanna parked further down and across the street from the address Sam had given her. She needed time for her nerves to settle. Sam and Mickey lived in a quiet, residential newly constructed part of town, within easy access to the college. Joanna could tell that the neighbourhood had been meticulously thought out to appeal to both single professionals and families. There were lots of trees and benches, and she was sure she spied a small park and playground at the end of the street. There were a few people out walking their dogs and pushing toddlers in strollers. The abundance of butterflies in her stomach showed no signs of resting their wings. She couldn't wait any longer, otherwise she would arrive late, but one last thing. She took the swan button out of her purse and squeezed it in her hand for good luck, then she grabbed the bottle of New Zealand Chardonnay which had been strongly recommended by the man in the wine shop, although she was sure she had detected that he spoke with an Antipodean accent. A bigger concern than the wine was her choice of dress. What would meet with the approval of a fashion designer other than one of his pieces? She hoped she didn't look too flamboyant in the cream shift with a gold leaf applique running along the side.

Sam was already holding the door open when she arrived, 'I saw you walking up the street. Come on inside.'

Mickey was sitting cross legged on the sofa, wearing a feather boa. 'Sam told me that you are a fan of Marc Bolan, so I wore this just for you.'

Joanna smiled, 'You do bear an uncanny resemblance.'

'So I've been told on numerous occasions, but people say I'm prettier.' Mickey jumped up and took the bottle of wine from her. 'I'll just put this in the fridge. Nice dress.'

Mickey didn't immediately return from the kitchen and Joanna was relieved to have more time alone with Sam. Mickey had made her feel awkward and shy, but she was sure it was because she had already convinced herself that she wouldn't meet with his approval. Did he really like her dress? She was annoyed with herself that it mattered. She was here because of Sam and he was as relaxed and easy going as always. He had a vast vinyl record collection, stored on brightly painted shelves in the living room, which he proudly showed her. They heard the timer go off in the kitchen and Sam went to serve dinner.

'Make yourself comfortable at the table. Sit anywhere. Tonight's meal is Mickey's choice,' Sam yelled from the kitchen.

Mickey appeared in the dining room. 'Yes, one of my favourites from when we were in Italy. I'm sure Sam has told you all about our time there.'

'Not too much, but he has sent me some of the music.'

'It's a very romantic country. Isn't that right, Sam?'

Sam came in carrying plates of delicious food. He didn't answer.

The wine flowed and the conversation was pleasant, but although Joanna did her best to relax, there was something about Mickey that bothered her. It was underlying and she couldn't put her finger on it.

'So, JOAnNAh, what did you think of the fashion show?' Mickey asked. They had finished eating and were sitting in the living room drinking cappuccinos.

'I loved it, especially the pink dress with the feathers.'

'Would you like to see it up close and personal?'

Mickey didn't give her the time to answer, he was already out of his seat and leading the way. He gestured for Joanna to follow. He led her upstairs and into a large, bright and airy room at the rear of the house, which he introduced as his workroom and sanctuary. One wall was covered in sketches, while another showcased magazine articles and photos. Hanging on a rack by his desk was the dress. It looked even more beautiful than she remembered. The way the sequins glistened and the feathers swayed in the breeze from the ceiling fan made it look as though it was dancing by itself. She thought she would give anything to be able to wear it. How wonderful to be able to enter a room, on Sam's arm, dressed in Mickey's pièce de résistance.

She made herself come back to earth and said, 'It is even more lovely than I remembered.'

Mickey gave a smile of self-satisfaction. 'Yes, I do think I rather outdid myself with this one, but onward and upward!' He sat down at his desk and made it obvious that he had work to do and she should now make herself scarce.

Joanna found Sam waiting for her at the bottom of the stairs.

'I really should be getting home. Thank you for a wonderful evening.'

She went to take her car keys out of her purse and noticed that her house key was missing. Sam noticed her look of consternation.

'Is something wrong?'

'Oh, it's nothing. I must have forgotten my door key. I keep a spare underneath a rock by the back door. Abigail painted it in pre-school. Rather silly really because it stands out a mile.'

Sam took her arm, 'Let me walk you to your car.'

Joanna wished she had parked further away; she didn't want him to take his leave of her.

When they reached her car, Sam looked thoughtful for a moment and then said, 'You don't have to let me know now, but I'm giving a lecture on the Eurovision Song Contest at the end of the month. It will be at the college and, afterwards, there will be a bit of a party with drinks and nibbles, and we'll be playing Eurovision entries requested by the audience.'

In her mind, Joanna was jumping up and down with excitement, 'I'll be there. Thank you.'

'Great. I'll send you the details and you think about the song you want to hear.'

'I don't even have to think about it, Estonia's entry from 2015, "Goodbye to Yesterday".'

'Really? That's one of my favourites, too. It should have won.'

Joanna couldn't restrain herself, 'I can't believe how much we have in common.'

She thought this was the perfect moment for their first kiss but it seemed as though Sam pulled back, albeit awkwardly. Rather too hurriedly he said goodbye and turned and left before she had even opened the car door.

Sam didn't look back; he was already dreading telling Mickey that he had invited Joanna to the Eurovision evening. He really should have run it by him first. When he got home, Mickey was in the dining room finishing the last of the wine.

'I invited Joanna to the Eurovision evening,' Sam blurted out rather too quickly.

Mickey slowly finished his glass and there was an awkward pause before he replied. 'You know what they say, three's a crowd!'

'I know, I'm sorry, I should have run it by you first.'

'Well, it's done now. I am sure JOAnNAh was over the moon at your invitation.'

Mickey was right, Joanna was over the moon, but she couldn't shake the feeling that things were not going to go as straightforward as she would have liked.

Joanna couldn't have been more excited than if she had been attending the Eurovision Song Contest itself. In fact, she was sure the atmosphere pretty much mirrored the live event. When she arrived, she was given a piece of paper on which to write her name and favourite Eurovision song. Once completed, the slips of paper were put into a jar to be given later to the DJ for the after show party. She entered the auditorium and saw that it was decked out with flags from the participating countries and at everyone's seat there was a mini flag to wave. She checked her flag's design on her phone to see which country it represented and was thrilled to discover it was Estonia. Sam thought of everything. She picked up her programme with the running order of events and saw that Mickey was also scheduled to give a talk on Eurovision fashion. Meeting Mickey again didn't faze her. She had taken the day off from work and had her hair done. She hadn't intended to buy something new to wear for the evening, but on her way home from the hairdressers, she stopped in one of her favourite boutiques and found the perfect dress. Since meeting Sam, she had lost weight and the body skimming silver cocktail dress she tried on was perfect in every way. Without any hesitation she bought it. As intended, it boosted not only her allure but her confidence. She had also scheduled the following day off from work, just in case she was late home or not home at all. Yes, tonight was destined to be the night.

Sam walked out onto the stage to the sound of Abba's "Waterloo" and was greeted with thunderous applause. He began by talking about the very first contest in 1956, and continued through the years, discussing the songs, the artists, each individual country's selection process, as well as referencing the political climate of the time. At the conclusion of each segment, TV clips from the years discussed were shown on a screen. Then it was Mickey's turn. He walked on stage, dressed from head to toe in blue satin. It was designed to be reminiscent of Abba's victory in 1974, but to Joanna he looked even more like Marc Bolan. He was wearing glitter under his eyes too; Metal Guru meets his Waterloo she jokingly thought. Mickey injected a lot of fun and humour into his topic, which wasn't hard to do, as many of the outfits were very outlandish. He had the audience both laughing and captivated. He truly was a showman. When it was over, the audience were shepherded into a large, adjacent banqueting area where a bar and buffet were set. The DJ was at the far end, still reading the requests from earlier and compiling a playlist. It was a packed house. The first strains of music were heard and a loud cheer erupted from a corner of the room. Joanna looked over and saw Mickey surrounded by adoring students.

'That's Mickey's fan club. Current fashion students.' Sam was standing next to her.

'I like the song that's playing. I've heard her voice before.' Joanna wasn't sure what was beating faster, the music or her heart.

'You have, it's Emma Marrone. Hers is one of the Italian tracks I sent you. She represented Italy in 2014. Mickey's favourite. He wants to design for her one day. Can I get us both a drink?'

Joanna couldn't help herself, she reached across and linked her arm in his. 'Thank you, but not just yet,' she said softly.

They were still locked together when a whirlwind of blue satin swooped across and grabbed Sam's other arm.

'Hello, JOAnNAh, are you enjoying our little soiree?' Mickey held on tightly.

'Why don't we all go over to the bar? I expect we would all enjoy a drink,' Sam asked rather unconvincingly and not waiting for an answer. He didn't want things to escalate any further. He managed to extricate himself from Joanna, much to her chagrin, but Mickey continued to hold onto Sam's arm and led them both across the room leaving Joanna to follow behind. The bar was crowded and she found herself separated and standing amidst a sea of strangers. Not even her perfectly coiffed hair or alluring dress could remedy the situation. What made it worse was that Sam didn't seem to notice, he didn't even bother to look for her. She reached in her purse and pulled out the swan button. She squeezed it hard in her hand and closed her eyes momentarily. Please don't let the evening continue this way, she prayed silently. At that moment the DJ chose to play her song, and it was not only her Eurovision request that was answered, seemingly out of nowhere Sam appeared by her side without Mickey, and handed her a glass of wine.

'Here, you could probably use this.' He gave her the glass. 'Sorry to have left you alone for so long. It was a mob scene. Mickey's holding court again.'

He gestured to where Mickey was once again surrounded by eager protegees. Even so, Joanna could feel Mickey watching them.

As if sensing what her next question might be, Sam offered, 'Mickey and I have known each other for a few years now. We're very close.' Why couldn't he just be honest and tell her he was gay, he silently asked himself, realising that he didn't know the answer.

Joanna held on to his response and remained in denial. Sam and Mickey were obviously close friends. If it had been anything more, Sam would have said. He had the perfect opportunity. Even though the truth, disguised in blue satin, was staring her in the face from the other side of the room, she refused to acknowledge it. She and Sam were meant to be together, never missing a beat as they danced through life to the music they loved almost as much as each other.

Joanna caught Mickey looking over again and realised that he was not going to give them many more opportunities to be alone. She needed to act quickly while she still had Sam to herself.

'I need to get going, I have to be up early for work,' she lied. 'Would you like to come over one evening next week and I'll return the favour and cook you dinner? I'll introduce you to my vinyl record collection. I have a lot of original Marc Bolan.'

She tried to make it all sound very casual. She was relieved when he seemed genuinely pleased and accepted her invitation.

'I'd love to. Tell me the date and I'll be there.'

'How about next Thursday? Shall we say 7:30?'

'Perfect. I'll be there with a bottle.'

'See you then. Please say goodbye to Mickey for me.'

She turned and quickly left, she didn't want to leave room for any awkward "shall I/shan't I" gestures of emotion.

Joanna arrived home earlier than anticipated and decided to call Abigail and tell her all about the evening. Abigail listened intently to all her mum was saying and also picked up on the details she conveniently failed to mention.

'Mum, I have to ask again if Sam's gay. This Mickey character sounds like he could be his boyfriend.'

'I know, Abbey, it's crossed my mind too, but there's definitely a chemistry between us.'

'Yes, but that chemistry could be a stick of dynamite about to blow up in your face.'

'Don't be silly. I know what I'm doing. Anyway, what about Tom Robinson?'

'Is that someone at work?'

'Don't be silly, Tom Robinson, the musician and broadcaster. He's gay, even released a song "Glad to be Gay" in the 70s, but now he's married to a woman and has a couple of kids. He describes himself as a gay man who happens to love a woman. So it can happen.'

'Mum, Sam isn't Tom Robinson.'

'No, he's Professor Sam McLaughlin and I'm in love with him and I know he has feelings for me. He's probably confused at the moment but he'll sort himself out.'

'I think you're the one who's confused and needs sorting out.'

'Oh Abbey, can't you at least be happy for me?'

'I'm trying, mum, I really am.'

'I've invited him over for dinner next Thursday. I'll let you know how it goes.'

'Okay, just don't get your hopes up. I love you,'

'Love you, too. Bye.'

Joanna suddenly felt exhausted. Before she got into bed, she took the swan button and put it under her pillow. She drifted off to sleep asking Lady Luck for a little extra help.

CHAPTER FIVE

Mickey reread the email he had just received. A few months ago, he had sent some sketches to Emma Marrone's manager and the reply was from her record company letting him know that they were interested in having Mickey design outfits for another of their artists, Giana, who was going to be presenting a six week series of shows on fashion and music called The Seen. They would see how this went and possibly have him design for Emma at a later date. He would be needed in Rome almost immediately and would probably have to initially stay for a month. Would Mickey be available for a Zoom call the next day? Why did this have to happen now? He needed to be here with Sam, not leave him wide open to more of Joanna's advances. Would a month in Italy be the end of his and Sam's relationship? Would Sam be able to take time away from teaching and go with him, more importantly would he want to? Rome held such very special memories for them both. He decided not to say anything until after the call. He found it hard to keep the news to himself, especially when Sam told him that he had been invited to Joanna's for dinner the following evening. Mickey worked long into the night, preparing for the next day's call. He did some research on Giana. She had been discovered at 16 years of age on a talent show. Still only 22, she was an established and popular singer songwriter and had even had some of her songs recorded by Emma. Mickey got the feeling that she was now trying to make a name for herself as a TV personality in an attempt to be considered more mature and to be taken more seriously. With this in mind, he drew some preliminary sketches of brightly coloured Chanel-esque suits, accentuated with fun and quirky trim. How he wished he still had the swan button.

Sam was getting ready to go and meet Joanna when Mickey eventually gave him the news. The record company loved his ideas and he was scheduled to fly out on Saturday.

'The only downside is I have to leave this weekend and then I'll be gone for a whole month, possibly a bit longer.'

For a fleeting moment Sam looked a little taken aback. Was he perhaps thinking how much they were going to miss each other or was he thinking about how much more time he could spend with Joanna? Mickey couldn't remember the last time he and Sam had been apart for longer than a weekend.

Sam appeared to compose himself, 'What a great opportunity. I can't say I'm surprised. Wow, Rome, wish I was going with you.'

'Why don't you come?'

'You won't want me there distracting you, plus I don't think the college would let me. We're at a pivotal section of the course.'

'I do want you there, Sam. Please try and convince the college to give you the time off. Even for just a couple of weeks.'

' Let me think about it. I have to run or I'll be late.'

And with that Sam left; a bottle of Prosecco in hand, while still holding his and Mickey's relationship in the balance.

As he drove to Joanna's, Sam tried to make sense of his emotions. He was thrilled for Mickey, and knew he was going to miss him, but he couldn't deny the sense of relief he felt when he thought about not having to explain himself every time he mentioned Joanna. Mickey had every right to feel jealous but Sam couldn't fully understand why. He was a gay man in a loving and fulfilling relationship so why did Joanna have this effect on him? By the time he reached the address Joanna had given him, he was no closer to an answer.

Joanna had changed the menu a dozen times. She had asked for suggestions from the people at work and decided on mushrooms stuffed with garlic butter to start, followed by moussaka. Baklava was for dessert.

She saw Sam walking up the front steps and opened the door, 'Welcome to my cottage.'

'Mmm, something smells good.'

'It's the moussaka.'

'It smells delish.'

'I hope it tastes as good as it smells. I don't find cooking easy. You could say it's all Greek to me!'

Sam gave her an easy smile and then stopped to read a wooden plaque hanging in the hallway, 'I may be old, but that's ok, I got to see Marc Bolan in concert!' he read aloud. This time he gave both an easy smile and an easy laugh.

'My daughter, Abigail, gave it to me for my birthday.'

'I love it. She has great taste, just like her mum.' He handed her the Prosecco.

'Thank you, I'll go put it in the fridge and check on the food. Why don't you make yourself comfortable in the living room?'

When she came back from the kitchen, Sam was knelt on the floor looking through her vinyl records.

'Wow, you have the 12" version of Dolce Vita by Ryan Paris. It was played all the time at the clubs in Italy when Mickey and I were there. I've a copy that's in the shape of a heart. It was released for Valentine's Day.'

'Would you like to hear it?'

'Actually, I'd love to hear this.' He handed her the Electric Warrior album by T. Rex. 'What's your favourite track?'

'All of them, but if I had to choose, it would be "Life's a Gas".'

Marc Bolan serenaded them throughout the evening. Just when Joanna thought things couldn't get any better, Sam told her about Mickey's upcoming trip to Rome and that he would be gone for at least a month. Yes, Joanna thought, all these nights of sleeping with the swan button under my pillow has worked its magic. I'll finally have you all to myself.

She couldn't stop herself when she said, 'I'll make sure you don't get too lonely.'

Sam didn't respond immediately. When he did, it wasn't exactly the reply she'd been hoping for. 'It's going to seem strange not having Mickey home. I can't remember the last time we spent more than a couple of days apart.'

'It sounds like a wonderful opportunity.'

'Yes, it is. He's always wanted to make a name for himself in Italy. Maybe his dream is about to come true. Actually, I hadn't realised how late it is. I'd better be going soon. I'm sure he needs help getting ready for the trip.'

Joanna tried her best not to show her disappointment at him leaving earlier than she'd planned. If she was truthful, she had hoped he wouldn't leave at all.

On his way out, he stopped and looked at the plaque again, 'So when is your birthday?'

'In less than two weeks, the 20th.'

'We'll have to do something to celebrate.'

'Yes, I'd love that.'

'Thanks for a wonderful evening. You're a superb cook.'

He gave her a chaste kiss on the cheek and was gone. Joanna hated that he was being too much of a gentleman.

When Sam arrived home, Mickey was sitting in his workroom surrounded by swatches of material.

'How was your evening?' Mickey didn't look up.

'Very nice, but I came home early in case you needed my help with anything.'

This time he did look up, 'Just your love, loyalty and support.'

'You'll always have those.'

'I'm going to hate being away from you, Sam.'

'I'm going to hate it, too, but the time will fly by. Come here.'

Sam held out his arms. Mickey ran into them and almost squeezed the breath out of him. After a few minutes, Sam loosened Mickey's grip and walked over to the pink sequined dress. It was still moving as though it had a life of its own. He knew this probably wasn't the right time to ask but he went ahead anyway.

'Mickey, are you ready to part with this? It's Joanna's birthday in a couple of weeks and I'd like to give it to her as a present.'

'Go ahead. It's so last season now anyway.' Mickey knew it wasn't a generous remark but he was hurt. He would have been flattered if it had been a gift for anyone else but Joanna. Just like the dress, he had to let it go. His only way of holding on to Sam was to play along in the hope that this obsession with Joanna would run its course. As difficult as it was, Mickey had to be patient and wait it out.

'Thanks, Mickey. I know she'll be so surprised and love it. I'll have to take her somewhere to celebrate where she can wear it.'

Mickey kept his head down and pretended to be sketching so Sam wouldn't see his tears.

'Are you okay?'

'I'm fine. Just tired. It's been a long day.'

'Why don't you come to bed. You still have all day tomorrow.'

'I'll be there soon. I just want to finish up this sketch.'

As soon as Sam left the room, Mickey let his tears fall freely. The demons had returned.

* * * * *

Joanna could hear "Life's a Gas" playing ever so softly. Why was the music still playing? She thought she had turned it off. She must have fallen asleep before she could do so. She tried to reach to silence the sound but her arms wouldn't move. They felt attached to some outside force. It took several laboured attempts but she finally managed to open her eyes. Out of the corner, she could see wires coming out of her arms. She looked like a puppet. It hurt to move her head and the bright light above was hurting her eyes again. Her hand grazed a sheet and the edge of whatever she was wearing. This definitely wasn't her bed and this didn't feel anything like her pink dress. She hoped it wasn't ruined. Was Abigail still here? She called her name, but she was so weak and her mouth so dry, her voice was inaudible. As her eyes slowly became accustomed to the layout of the room, she thought it resembled a hospital, but why, how? Bit by bit, she began to feel her strength start to slowly ebb away. She tried to hang on in case someone was there. She wanted them to know she was awake....had questions.....needed to speak to Abigail............

* * * * *

Mickey cleared customs at Rome's Leonardo da Vinci Airport and quickly found a taxi to take him to his hotel. On the way, he texted Sam to let him know he'd arrived safely. Once in his room, he took a photo of the view from his balcony and texted Sam again. He paced anxiously waiting for a reply. Would Sam remember the view and would it make him want to visit? Giana had had a bottle of Champagne delivered to his room with a friendly note saying how much she was looking forward to meeting him. He poured himself

39

a glass and looked at the room service menu. He didn't feel like going out to eat tonight. Sam replied that he wished he was there and he would see what he could do if Mickey had to stay longer. Mickey hoped he meant it. He spent the evening sitting in his room putting the finishing touches to his designs. He opened the door to his balcony in the hope that the lights and the sounds from outside would stop him from feeling so lonely. Eventually exhaustion, both physical and emotional, won. He fell asleep dreaming that he was chasing a man who was running away from him carrying a pink sequined dress. Eventually the man disappeared, leaving Mickey drained and unable to speak because his mouth was full of feathers.

Mickey wasn't meeting with Giana until Monday morning so he had the remainder of the weekend to himself. He spent the Sunday exploring Rome, revisiting the favourite places he had shared with Sam. Mickey was not religious. He had come close to having a faith as a child when he likened his story to Moses in the Bulrushes and imagined that his mother had accidentally given him away after she had hidden him to keep him safe, but now he found himself walking away from the crowds of tourists and into a medieval church. It was as though he had entered another world. It was hard to believe that such peace and calm could be found inside these doors when the frenetic pace of daily life was whirring, hidden, only a few metres away. He knelt down in a pew and prayed. He acknowledged that if there was a God this was the time and place to be heard, but he wasn't entirely convinced and, once outside, he tossed three coins in the Trevi Fountain for good measure.

The record company offices occupied a beautiful old villa on the outskirts of Rome. Everything about the architecture was an inspiration to Mickey. He loved the pattern on the tiles of the floor, and the smooth ridges on the pillars in the courtyard reminded him of pleats. As soon as he reached the conference room where he was to meet Giana, he began to sketch, incorporating these new ideas into his next collection of designs. Giana arrived a little late with her manager who made the introductions and then left.

They hit it off immediately when the first words out of Giana's mouth were, 'You're even prettier than me.'

As if in agreement, Mickey shook his curls and gave her his charismatic and cheeky grin. From that moment their friendship was sealed.

Giana was easy to dress; she was petite and stunning. She didn't wear, or need, much make-up to enhance her God given good looks and wore her natural brown hair mid-length. She could be versatile and was the perfect muse for Mickey's designs. She was an inspiration and they collaborated well. She was a born stylist and added a few of her own quirky accessories to Mickey's designs. Ordinarily, he would have demanded complete control, right down to the last hook and eye, but her ideas didn't look out of place, enhanced the clothes, and he found himself welcoming her input. He loved working with her and the feeling was mutual. They had an intense schedule, and within a few days, she had her complete wardrobe for the first few shows, with plenty more ideas for the next.

After they had recorded the first show, they went out to dinner to celebrate. Giana was wearing his cream leotard dress with the feather skirt but with a black leather jacket and biker boots. It was exactly the way Mickey would have styled it. He was in his element.

He was even more thrilled when she said, 'I want to include a segment on you and your designs in one of the shows. We'll do an interview as an informal chat and you can show some of your favourite pieces and describe the inspiration behind them. I think you're super talented.'

'I think you're pretty amazing yourself.' Mickey felt so at ease in her company. Was this how Sam felt when he was with Joanna? 'Do you have any brothers or sisters?'

'Not that I'm aware of but I'm adopted.'

'So am I.' He very rarely admitted it, but Mickey didn't even think before he spoke. He was surprised that the words came out so easily.

'Aren't we lucky that our mothers loved us so much, they allowed someone else to raise us in order to give us a better life?'

'I've never thought of it that way.'

'Haven't you? I'm surprised. Look at how super successful we are and it's all thanks to one of the most selfless acts of love known to womankind. I'm sure that a day doesn't go by when my birth mum isn't thinking about me and wondering how I'm doing. Imagine carrying and bonding with your child for nine months, giving birth and holding your precious bundle in your arms, knowing you are going to give your baby to another family because you want a better life and opportunities for them, something you are unable to give them yourself. That has to be the most selfless and loving act of all.'

41

Mickey was hanging on her every word. 'Feeling the way you do, have you ever tried to find your mum?'

'No, I'll let that be her decision. I think it's only fair. She's done enough for me already.'

Back at the hotel, Mickey wanted to call Sam, but it was a weeknight and he knew it was too late. He'd call him in the morning. He lay in bed and thought about the things Giana had said. As he began to drift into a deep and cathartic sleep, he was aware that he felt an inner peace, the likes of which he had never experienced before.

The next morning, Sam could sense a change in Mickey's mood and it was definitely for the better. He sounded so bright and positive on the phone. Mickey even asked what Sam had planned for Joanna's birthday. When he told him that they were going to celebrate on a Riverboat Disco, he even managed a lighthearted response.

'At least my dress will get a bloody good workout.'

'And tons of compliments. You sound as though you're enjoying yourself. Are things going well?'

'Yes, they are. Giana is a dream to collaborate with.'

'I'm so happy for you, Mickey, but don't enjoy yourself so much that you don't want to come home.'

Mickey was in a good place and could afford to be generous, but he didn't want Sam to get too complacent so he swiftly changed the subject.

'Giana is going to feature me and my designs on one of her shows. Who knows what doors that may open?'

'That's impressive. Perhaps I'd better plan on coming over.'

'I thought you couldn't get away. Anyway, it's entirely up to you.'

Mickey knew he was being flippant, but he felt that Sam deserved it. He might have made peace with his mother, but Joanna was another story.

CHAPTER SIX

It was less than a week until her birthday but Joanna didn't think she could wait any longer to see Sam again, especially as she knew that he was by himself with Mickey away in Rome. She decided to give him a call and casually suggest that they meet for lunch at a newly opened Greek restaurant near the college.

'You'll finally get to enjoy a proper authentic Greek meal.'

'I probably won't be able to taste the difference. In fact, we'll probably agree that your cooking's better.'

'I doubt it. This place has rave reviews.'

The weather was still nice so they sat outside. Sam acknowledged a few of his students sitting at another table. Joanna was secretly pleased and flattered that they appeared to be taking an interest in his dining companion.

She began the conversation by asking about Mickey, not that she especially wanted to know, but she thought it would appear rather obvious and rude if she didn't.

'How's Mickey getting on?'

'It's going really well. He loves designing for Giana. They seem to be kindred spirits.'

'Did you say she's also a singer?'

'Yes, and a songwriter. I'll send you some of her music.'

'Thank you, I would love that.'

'Have you ever written anything or performed?'

'Why do you ask?'

'You strike me as being creative, and with your passion for music, it wouldn't surprise me.'

'Well, Abigail says I have a very vivid imagination but she doesn't mean it in that way, but I will let you into a secret. Back in the '80's, I had this idea for a band. We were called "The Exotic Pets". Sadly, nothing came of it.'

'I'm intrigued, please tell me more.'

'We had aspirations to become the next Bananarama. It was me and two girlfriends.'

'Who came up with the name.'

'Me. I worked with a girl who kept small exotic animals. One day she referred to them as her exotic pets and I thought what a great name for a band.'

'Was your image similar to Bananarama?'

'Not at all. I was going through my Rita Hayworth phase so we wore 1940's inspired outfits.'

'What about songs?'

'I wrote them. I remember one was called Holly Would.' Joanna began to sing quietly but not self-consciously, 'And when he asks do you wanna, and she says I didn't oughta, he replies, let me tell you, Holly would.' We made a demo but then it all fizzled out.'

Sam's students had turned to look at them and he began to laugh.

Joanna looked quite hurt, 'Remember this was the '80s. We were pretty cool at the time.'

'I don't know about cool, I'd say you were pretty hot. I'm laughing because you never cease to surprise me. Joanna, you are absolutely amazing.'

Joanna was thrilled. She hoped he found her more amazing than Mickey, and did he also say hot? Her cup runneth over.

All too soon, it was time for them both to get back to work.

'Be ready at six on your birthday. I'll pick you up.'

'But where are we going? What should I wear?' Joanna wanted to be prepared.

'Both are a surprise. It's all taken care of.'

'Even what I'm wearing?'

'Especially what you're wearing.'

'But how will I ....'

'No more questions. I'll see you on the 20th.'

She watched him walk away and realised he was equally as attractive from the back as from the front. She noticed the students watching curiously. Joanna gave them a smug, confident smile and headed back to her office.

There was no doubt in Sam's mind that he was guilty of taking things further than intended. He just couldn't help himself. He found it hard to put on the brakes when it came to Joanna. She had such an effect on him. It was both cerebral and physical but not in a sexual way. He had never experienced anything like this before and he was at a loss to know how to handle it. He wanted Mickey for a lover and Joanna for a friend but he knew it was impossible, and unfair, to have them both. Mickey was already jealous and Joanna wanted a romantic involvement. He had given her every right to think that there was more on offer and tonight was no exception. He wanted to do something special for her birthday but had he gone too far? There was a knock at the door. It was the courier. Sam gave him the box addressed to 135 Coolgardie Avenue. Joanna should receive it in less than 30 minutes. He imagined her reaction and was overcome with guilt. There he went again, probably building her hopes up.

Joanna could not contain her excitement. She was the luckiest girl on the planet. This was going to be the best birthday ever.

An hour ago, a courier had delivered a large box. The card read, "This is for you to wear when we celebrate tonight. Pick you up at 6. Sam." She had hurriedly opened the lid and inside, wrapped in reams of tissue paper, was THE dress, a cornucopia of pink sequins and feathers. She immediately tried it on. She had wondered if it would be uncomfortable to wear. Not that it would have stopped her, but she needn't have been concerned. The lining was made of very soft fabric and it felt and looked a dream, her dream come true. She still couldn't believe the dress was hers but, more importantly, she couldn't believe she was going to be wearing the dress on a date with Sam. She promised herself that she would always wear it in joy and in love.

Sam arrived early but she had been ready for more than an hour. When he saw her, there was no doubt in his mind that he had done the right thing in giving Joanna the dress. She looked stunning. Even Mickey would have approved.

Joanna was the first to speak, 'Hello, Prince Charming. Your Cinderella is ready to go to the ball. Actually, you're my Prince Charming and Fairy Godmother all rolled into one.'

'That dress was made for you. It's perfect.'

'Thank you so much, and Mickey too. It must have been hard for him to give it up.' Joanna wondered if Mickey had put up a fight. If he had, Sam didn't let on.

'He knew it was going to someone who would appreciate it. That's all that mattered.'

'Where are we going? I hope I won't be overdressed.'

'Don't you worry. You're going to be the belle of the ball.'

They had been driving for almost 30 minutes and Joanna still had absolutely no idea what Sam had planned. If she was truthful, she really didn't care; McDonalds would have been fine, just as long as she got to celebrate her birthday and spend the evening with him, although her dress would have probably looked a little out of place at a fast food restaurant. She began to recognise landmarks and realised they were approaching the river. In the distance, she saw the lights of the pier. Sam parked close by and took her hand. She now saw fairy lights and the outlines of a boat. She could hear music, her kind of music.

Sam ushered her along a boarding ramp, 'Cinders, we are going to celebrate your birthday on a riverboat disco. Your carriage awaits.'

Joanna found herself sitting at a table for two, with a perfect view of the buildings along the embankment as they reflected the city lights onto the water. A bottle of Champagne was already chilled and waiting. They had just ordered appetizers when the DJ started playing Kylie's "Can't Get You Out of My Head".

'Shall we? I want everyone to see you shimmy in your dress.'

Joanna hesitated for a second. She had never possessed or worn a dress like this one before. Was it too much? Would the other people laugh? She needn't have worried. When Sam pushed back his chair and led Joanna on to the dance floor, all doubt was gone. She couldn't remember the last time she had had a willing dance partner. Mark had always sat in a corner, until it became apparent that he stuck out more like a sore thumb if he remained there, rather than join his wife and move to the music as best he could. That's what he liked about Genesis and Floyd, you could just sit. Nothing more was expected of you other than to listen and occasionally nod your head. The song ended and Sam and Joanna returned to their table for food and drinks.

Lots more dancing followed and then the DJ stopped the music and announced that it was Joanna's birthday. A cake was brought out as everyone sang "Happy Birthday". Sam then led her once more to the dance floor and the DJ played Sam's special request, "Happy Birthday" by Altered Images.

All too quickly the evening was drawing to a close and the last song was being played, a slow number, the anthemic "Hey There Lonely Girl" by Eddie Holman. Couples were dancing and Joanna waited for Sam to invite her on to the floor again, but he didn't, and something told her not to ask. It was the only disappointment to an otherwise perfect night.

During the drive home, Joanna rested her head on Sam's shoulder, feigning sleep. She longed for him to stroke her hair, or provide some form of physical contact, but it was not forthcoming. Sam sensed her need and knew that the time was fast approaching when he would have to be brutally honest. She was making it blatantly apparent that she wanted more than friendship. When they reached her house, he declined her invitation to come in and made the excuse that he had an early class in the morning.

Once home, Sam addressed his dilemma. He had done his best, but now was the time to pull away. He was missing Mickey's company more than he thought possible. He didn't want to lose Mickey and his absence highlighted the fact that he had come close and he had treated him unfairly when it came to Joanna. What a mess he had made of things. He had hurt Mickey and he was now about to hurt Joanna.

Joanna took off the dress and hung it carefully on the outside of her wardrobe. When she opened her eyes in the morning, she wanted it to be the first thing she saw. A reminder that she had just spent the most perfect evening of her life.

Sam needed to act fast. He couldn't put it off any longer. It made no sense to wait as there was never going to be a good time. He texted Joanna and asked if she fancied meeting for lunch in the park. He thought the park would be an ideal location. He hoped she wouldn't get too upset, but if things got too bad, he could leave quickly without worrying about waiting to pay a restaurant bill.

He saw Joanna before she noticed him. She was sitting on a bench, feeding a friendly squirrel a piece of her sandwich. She was such a lovely person, and although necessary, this was going to be very hard to do.

Sam's approaching footsteps caused the squirrel to run away and Joanna to look up, 'Have you brought something for lunch?'

Sam realised that he'd been so distracted thinking about how to say what had to be said that he'd completely forgotten to bring something to eat. 'I was famished earlier so I've already eaten,' he lied.

'I haven't yet given all of my sandwich to the squirrel. I don't think he'll mind if I share the rest with you.'

'Thank you, but it's okay. I'm still full.'

He sat down and Joanna moved closer. It was now or never.

'Joanna, we have to talk. There's something that needs to be said and I should have said it sooner.'

'Is it about us?'

'Yes, it is. I want you to........'

'It's alright, I already know and I completely understand.'

'You do?'

'Yes. You made it very clear from the start.'

'I did?'

'Yes, and I think you've handled everything really well, considering.'

'Well thank you. It hasn't been easy. I've never been in this situation before.'

'You made it very obvious on my birthday. That was all the proof I needed.'

Sam thought she was referring to the drive home, when he hadn't responded when she put her head on his shoulder and made it clear that she expected more than friendship.

'I had the best birthday ever and it was all because of you.'

'I'm glad you enjoyed yourself.'

'I did, I just feel bad for Mickey. You two are very close. Perhaps Giana has a friend.'

'I'm sorry, Joanna, but I'm not sure I get your meaning.'

'Mickey. Or haven't you told him about us yet? Of course, silly me, you're probably waiting until he gets back from Italy.'

Sam was at a loss for words. They had been talking at cross purposes the entire time and now the situation was even worse. He had built her hopes up even more. He didn't know what to say next. All he could think about was getting away. He made a pretence of looking at the time.

'I have to go. I have a class starting in fifteen minutes.' And with that, he was gone.

Joanna had hoped for a kiss or some outward show of affection but she convinced herself it was probably because they were in a public place and close to the college.

She got out her phone and called Abigail, 'Abbey, I was right all along. It's Tom Robinson all over again.'

Abigail didn't immediately get her meaning, 'Tom Robinson?'

'Yes, Sam has fallen in love with me.'

'Has he said something?'

'Not in so many words. He still has to tell Mickey.'

'So, Mickey is, sorry was, his boyfriend?'

'I'm not sure. I just know they are very close. But it doesn't matter because Sam wants to be with me.'

'It all sounds rather complicated.'

'Please be happy for me.'

'I am, mum, I just don't want you to get hurt.'

'How can I? Sam has made it very clear that he wants to be with me.'

'Okay, whatever you say. I hope you're not reading too much into this.'

'I'm not. We arranged to meet in the park and that's when he told me.'

'How romantic.' Abigail tried not to sound sarcastic.

'What are you doing after work this evening?'

'Nothing. Going straight home.'

'Then stop by. I'll open a bottle of Prosecco and we can celebrate.'

'Sure. I'll be there around six.'

'Great. I'll see you then. Love you.'

'Love you too.'

Joanna noticed the squirrel was back, 'Here, have it all. I'm feeling generous.'

She not only gave him the rest of her sandwich but her packet of crisps as well.

Abigail arrived with a bottle of Champagne. 'It can be a double celebration. We just won a big case.'

'Congratulations. I'm so very proud of you.'

Abigail couldn't help but notice how much younger and vibrant her mother looked. She now exuded a love of life that was contagious and so was her smile.

'This Sam obviously agrees with you.'

'Abbey, I can't remember the last time I've felt this happy. In fact, I don't remember ever being this happy.'

'Not even in the early days with dad?'

Her daughter's remark caught Joanna off guard. How could she have been so thoughtless? No matter how she now felt about Mark, he was still Abigail's father and someone that her daughter loved very much.

She tried to soften her previous comment, 'Well, yes, of course your dad made me happy but it's hard to remember that far back.' It wasn't working, she was making matters worse, it was obvious from the look on Abigail's face. There was only one thing for it, 'I'll go get us our drinks.'

'So, what were Sam's exact words to you today?' Abigail yelled into the kitchen.

'It was more a case of what he didn't say. I could just tell.' Joanna returned to the living room with two glasses of bubbling Moet. 'Here's to the two of us and our incredible futures.'

'Are you sure you're not getting ahead of yourself? You haven't known him very long.'

'Abbey, what more can I say to convince you? Sam arranged to meet in the park today because he wanted to talk about our relationship.'

'Did he tell you that he loved you? Wanted to be with you?'

'Not in so many words but I know that's what he meant.'

'Mum, perhaps he wanted to talk to you about Mickey.'

'He did but only because he doesn't want to hurt him. They're very close.'

'Mum, do I have to spell it out? Sam is gay and he isn't this Tom Robinson you keep going on about.'

Joanna put her glass down on the table with such force that some of her Champagne spilled.

'Do I have to spell it out to you? Sam and Mickey are over. Sam wants to be with me.'

'I'll believe it when I see it. I'm afraid it is already too late but please don't get your hopes up.'

Abigail thought it best that she leave before she said something she might regret.

Joanna had to bite her tongue, too. Instead, she said, 'Darling, I'm sorry. I keep forgetting how hard our divorce must be on you. Your father is a good, kind man.'

'Mum, that's not it at all. I just think that all Sam can offer you is friendship but you've made it very clear to me that you want more.'

'Then we'll have to agree to disagree but please try and be happy for me.'

'I will say that you look wonderful but I want you to stay that way and not get hurt.'

'Don't worry. I know what I'm doing.' Joanna reached out for a hug.

'I hope so mum. I really do.'

Abigail hugged her mother goodbye, aware that their roles were now reversed, but she knew that Joanna was a grown woman and, try as she might, she would be unable to protect her.

Sam was going to try for a second time. He booked a table at a restaurant that would afford them some privacy and texted Joanna the time and place. He hoped she wouldn't be too angry and hurt when he told her the truth but he couldn't blame her if she was. He really should have stuck to his guns and continued on and told her when they met at the park. Instead, he'd chosen to run away. It hadn't been fair to either of them. While Sam had a heavy heart, Joanna was ecstatic. It had only been three days since they'd last met and now Sam wanted to see her again. She was sure he wanted to meet because he couldn't keep his feelings to himself any longer. He must be officially going to tell her that he loved her over a romantic dinner. She took out the swan button and kissed it. It had brought her luck every time so far. She wasn't even sure that any more was needed. She loved him and he loved her. Cinderella was going to have her fairytale ending.

Sam was already on his second cocktail; for Dutch courage he told himself, and, boy, did he need it. This had been going on for too long, never quite saying what he really meant. Always holding back that one sentence that would have made all the difference. Always a dance of merry quips, when purposeful, choreographed steps were called for. He had made up his mind that tonight was going to be definitive. It was only fair. They both deserved it. But where was Joanna? Suppose she wasn't coming, had gone over their conversation in the park and guessed the real reason for dinner, and wasn't ready to hear what had already been staring her in the face all along? Would it have been smarter, kinder to them both, to have planned the evening in a more intimate setting, perhaps cooked dinner at home? She always said he was an excellent cook. He must stop all of this second guessing right now, it was driving him to drink when what he was about to say needed a clear head, not to mention a coherent tongue.

He had just downed the last of his drink when Joanna arrived. She looked as lovely as ever, a flurry of excuses and excitement as she apologised for being held up in traffic, what did he think of her hair, her dress, and that she'd heard the cedar plank salmon was to die for.

'As long as you don't eat the cedar plank,' was his futile attempt at a joke. He had known she would laugh. She did every time, and now he was about to wipe the smile off her face, forever. 'Joanna, I...'

'Are you ready to order, Sir?' He hadn't noticed the waiter approach.

'Could you please give us a few more minutes?'

'Of course, Sir.'

'Joanna...'

'Please hurry up and decide what you want. I'm starving.' Joanna put down her menu and beckoned to the waiter, who appeared again at their table in a flash.

No sooner had they ordered, than she stood up and announced she was going to the loo. While she was gone, a bottle of wine arrived and, against his better judgement, Sam poured them each a large glass, knowing that he really shouldn't have any more to drink. He had known this wasn't going to be easy but each interruption made it harder. Every time his carefully chosen words were poised on the tip of his tongue, they toppled backwards, choking and rendering him speechless.

Joanna returned and raised her glass, 'Here's to us. I can't believe how fate brought us together. I'm so lucky to have met you.'

Sam took a huge gulp of his wine and then poured more. He was rapidly losing his bottle in more ways than one. It was now or never. 'Joanna, there's someth.....'

She reached for his hand and got there before he could finish with the words he absolutely did not want to hear, 'Sam, I love you.'

She had beaten him to it. It should not have come as a surprise, he had guessed all along, but her never speaking the words until now, not saying them out loud, had produced an ethereal effect. He had almost hoped their lightness would somehow cause them to blow away but now they were out there for all the world to hear and, although said softly, were hard and set in stone. Too much alcohol, rather than strengthen his resolve, was blurring the lines. Was he sure he still wanted to go through with this? She had left him no choice.

This time it was he who reached for her hand, held her expectant gaze, and readied himself to respond with words for which she was neither prepared nor expecting, 'Let's eat.'

CHAPTER SEVEN

Sam knew his suitcase had seen better days but so had he. Both had begun to show signs of wear and tear. The baggage tags from his previous trip were still attached. As he removed them, he smiled at the memories they evoked. It would be good to be back, no matter the circumstance.

What to take? There was no time to do laundry but, thankfully, he still had plenty that was appropriate and clean. Luckily, he didn't need to pack too much. He meticulously chose item by item of clothing until the pieces were all laid out on the bed. Most places were casual so he wouldn't need a suit, just as well because he only had the one and he remembered, too late, that it was still at the dry cleaners. He placed a smart pair of jeans and a cream linen jacket in the case. A couple of black, white and navy t-shirts followed. He did plan to have some fun, so he added his Kylie shirt with the slogan 'Your Disco Needs You', plus two more pairs of jeans; one pair well-worn and another in white. He packed a pair of loafers or, as he preferred to call them, his dancing shoes. He would wear his trainers to travel in, and once there, for cushioning the cobbles as he walked around the city streets. The shoes still looked new, which reminded him that it would be the most exercise he had taken in quite a while. As a consequence, he wondered if the white jeans were going to feel a little snug, but he couldn't be bothered to pull them out of the case to make sure. Underwear and toiletries were next. As an afterthought, he reached far into the back of his wardrobe. Any further and he would have entered Narnia. He pulled out a slightly creased dress shirt and a tie, in the unlikely event he rediscovered his religion and visited a church, but perhaps if his prayers were answered........

It had already turned dark and there was a chill in the air. It reminded him of how cold it might feel on the plane, so he grabbed a sweater. He placed his passport and ticket in his designer leather travel organizer, a recent birthday present from Mickey. He remembered the look of horror and how Mickey had chastised him for carrying his important travel documents in a bum bag. He felt the first murmurs of possible excitement. Mickey would be so pleased to see him using the organizer. Might it help him realise that home is where the heart is? There was still room in the case. Sam walked throughout the house and found the perfect memento: a framed, red, heart shaped vinyl record of Dolce Vita by Ryan Paris. He swaddled it in t-shirts.

The case was closed, but just for good measure, Sam slid three coins into his pocket. When he arrived at his destination, he would use them for luck.

Twenty-four hours later Sam arrived at the Palazzo Hotel in Rome. He had told the college there was a family emergency which was the truth if you bent it a little. He made his way to Mickey's room and knocked on the door unannounced. He was counting on Mickey assuming he was from room service and answering the door. He needn't have worried, within seconds he was staring at Mickey's gorgeous face for the first time in almost a month. If Mickey was surprised to see him, he didn't let on, and a small smile began to appear.

Sam held out his arms, 'When you're ready, I'm here to take you home.'

Mickey didn't say a word. He just grabbed Sam's arm and pulled him into the room. He closed the door and gave Sam the biggest hug and kiss he had ever known. They held each other tight for what seemed like hours.

Twenty-four hours later and Joanna was distraught and humiliated. The evening had begun so full of promise. She had been certain that if she told Sam how she felt, he would tell her that he felt the same way. Granted, she was old school and had hoped that he would declare his feelings first but perhaps he needed a nudge in the right direction; she had not expected a complete U-turn. In her case the U stood for UNHAPPY, all upper case.

It had been impossible to continue the meal with her declaration of love unaddressed, so she had pressed him for an answer. She could not only see, but feel him squirm, until he couldn't delay the inevitable any longer. When he eventually replied, she wished she had never asked.

'I'm sorry, Joanna, there's no easy way to say this knowing how you feel, but I can only offer friendship. Nothing of a romantic kind.'

'I don't understand, Sam. I thought we shared something special.'

'We do, a special friendship, but I'm gay. I'm in a relationship with Mickey and I intend to spend the rest of my life with him. I'm sorry, I should have told you all of this sooner, but I thought it was obvious. I wrongly assumed you knew.'

How had it all gone so wrong? What about Tom Robinson? It was not only the salmon that had remained virtually untouched on her plate; her appetite for life was gone.

She needed to get out and she also needed groceries. She didn't think she would ever feel like eating again, definitely not salmon, but perhaps being amongst people and the bustle of the supermarket might help lift her mood. She needed a sense of purpose and she had to start somewhere. Restocking her pantry was as good a place as any.

She hadn't prepared a list and she pushed her empty cart aimlessly up and down the aisles. She had to get a grip or she would be completely off her trolley. As she wandered the fresh produce section, she became aware that Phil Collins was serenading her with "One More Night". When had Phil Collins been relegated to supermarket music? It was too much and she couldn't prevent the tears. She noticed people staring at her. Realising she was standing by a mountain of onions, she explained herself.

'Onions always make me cry.'

'I thought that was only when you peeled them,' remarked one concerned shopper.

'Oh no, some types are especially strong.'

It was a feeble excuse, she knew. She moved over to the corner and feigned interest in some cucumbers. What would they play next, The Pretenders, "Stop your Sobbing"?

Arriving home shaken and empty handed, Joanna read for the umpteenth time the text Sam had sent her.

Joanna, I apologise for the obvious hurt I've caused you. I'll be in Italy for the next couple of weeks. I'll be in touch when I return. I do hope we can still be friends.

All at once she knew what she must do, and meticulously began to plan her next step.

CHAPTER EIGHT

Mickey couldn't wait to introduce Sam to Giana. 'This is Sam, the love of my life.'

Giana was having her hair and make-up done for the recording of her next show. She couldn't turn around, so greeted him through the mirror.

'It's nice to finally meet you, Sam. I hope you'll stay for the show.'

'I'd be delighted to.'

Mickey was fussing with his designs, so Sam wandered out and found a seat in the audience. The recording wasn't scheduled for another hour, but there was someone else sitting a few seats away and he introduced himself as the PR Manager for Giana's record company. An easy conversation followed. By the time Mickey had joined them, Sam had been given a business card and told to call if he ever found himself in Rome and needed a job.

'What was all that about?' Mickey asked.

'He said they could use me in their Film and TV licensing department. They also send people out to the colleges to speak to students who are looking for a career in the music industry. What do you think, Mickey? Do you think we both have a future here in Rome?'

Before Mickey could answer, Giana took the stage. The show was about to begin.

Sam thought Giana suited Mickey's designs beautifully, and she was a natural as a presenter and interviewer. Towards the end of the show, she invited Mickey onto the set with her.

'This is Mickey Harman, the man behind the wonderful outfits I am wearing. He designed each and every one, and next week he will be my special guest. I want you all to know him better and learn more about the inspiration behind his clothes.'

The two embraced as the fade out music began and the credits rolled.

Giana and Mickey were all smiles as they came over and joined Sam.

'I am having the best time,' Giana said excitedly, 'and meeting Mickey is the icing on the cake. I'm so sad that next week is the final show.'

'I'm sure they'll renew the series. You're a natural.' Sam meant every word.

'Thank you, Sam. I'm glad you were able to make it. I'm going to leave you two lovebirds to enjoy the rest of the day together, I'm sure you have a lot of catching up to do and places to explore. Enjoy our beautiful city.'

'We will. I'll see you for the next recording, and my TV debut.'

'Your debut just happened, Mickey, and I'm sure you'll have hordes of fans when it airs tomorrow.'

Mickey was in his element. Giana brought out the best in him.

Italy had been kind to them once before. Sam and Mickey had already been living together for two years when they decided to spend a year in Milan and Rome. It was the time spent here that cemented their relationship. It took the ruins of past disappointments and made them whole again. Wandering the galleries and museums, they learnt the art of trust. Both found new inspiration for their passions, including each other. This time did not look as though it would disappoint either. It was obvious to Sam that Mickey was in a good place, both mentally and metaphorically. Sam wasn't sure if it was his decision to join him in Rome or if it was Giana. If it was Giana, he was eternally grateful to her.

They ended up at a restaurant they had frequented before. There was no doubt in Sam's mind that he had done the right thing by coming to Rome and surprising Mickey.

'This place agrees with you. You're the happiest I've seen you in a long time.'

Mickey's response was without words, just an impish grin.

'I think Italy agrees with us both,' Sam continued. 'I, for one, wouldn't mind giving it a try living here.'

This time his remark threw Mickey off guard.

'Honestly? What about leaving Joanna?' Mickey was mad at himself for mentioning her, but at least he didn't ridicule her name this time.

'Mickey, please believe me when I say that I'm sorry for any hurt I might have caused you. I told her that I'm gay and that I want to spend the rest of my life with you. She and I can be friends, but that's as far as it goes.'

'Perhaps we could make a fresh start here?'

'Yes, why not? I'm sure you're going to make a name for yourself with your designs for Giana and I can reach out to my contact at her record company. I have a good feeling about this '

'It sounds like a brilliant plan and I have a good feeling about us.' Mickey picked up his wine glass, 'A toast to us.'

On their way back to the hotel, they passed the church that Mickey had visited when he first arrived.

'Stay here, Sam, I won't be long.'

Sam watched as Mickey entered the church. He wasn't gone long.

'What was all that about?'

'I wanted to say thank you.'

The sun was starting to set and they were embraced by the large shadow of the church. Sam turned Mickey around to face him and took both of his hands in his.

'Mickey Harman, will you please do me the honour of marrying me?'

Mickey did not hesitate with his reply, 'Professor Sam McLaughlin, I thought you'd never ask. Yes! And I get to design my own dress.'

Mickey and Giana were spending the whole day being photographed for a ten page spread in a high class, popular glossy magazine, primarily showcasing Mickey's designs. The article was also going to feature an interview with them both. It was a major coup and they both found it difficult to contain their excitement. Each time Giana appeared wearing a different outfit, the magazine staff, especially the editor, went into raptures, and the photographer was in his element. The magazine shoot was also being filmed for a segment to be included in a popular evening entertainment programme. Mickey and Giana both knew that their careers were about to be propelled into the fast lane.

While Mickey was busy with his photoshoot, Sam decided to take the tram to Monteverde, a residential neighbourhood outside of Rome. If they were going to move here, they needed to decide where they wanted to live. After he had passed some shops and restaurants, he reached a park which was overlooked by a number of apartment buildings. One that was cream fronted with dark green wooden shutters especially caught his eye. As he approached the gate, some people were leaving. Noticing his interest, one of the men in the group asked if he would like to see inside? The garden flat was for rent and the invitation was from the landlord. Although small inside, the natural light made it appear more spacious. Patio doors opened onto a paved garden, perfect as neither Sam nor Mickey enjoyed maintaining a lawn. In fact, a window box was too much for Mickey to tend. To add greenery, there were a number of hanging flower baskets. It was a small outside space, but big enough to allow for a round table and two chairs. Sam could visualise the two of them spending evenings sitting outside, Mickey sketching, while they both shared a bottle of wine. The landlord pointed out that they weren't far from the beach at Ostia, perfect for weekend visits, although Sam rather imagined that they would probably vacation on Capri. Sam thanked his guide, gratefully accepted his card, and went to find some lunch. He liked the ambience of the town and thought that Mickey would too. Everything was starting to come together.

Mickey had found it hard to keep the wedding news to himself, but decided to wait until the end of the photoshoot to tell Giana, so he could give it his full, dramatic effect.

He began by asking her if she would be his bridesmaid.

'Whaaaat? Has Sam proposed?'

'Yes, at long last.'

'You bet I'll be your bridesmaid. I never pass up a chance to wear a beautiful dress, especially one designed by you.' She threw her arms around him and gave him a big hug. 'Think about holding the ceremony on Capri. It is beautiful and my Aunt has a house there. I'm sure she'd let you use it. Oh yes, and one last thing, instead of confetti, I'm going to throw glitter.'

The final show had been recorded, which included Mickey's interview, and a second series was already being discussed. Mickey and Sam were scheduled to fly home the next day, so Sam suggested they spend their last day in Monteverde.

As he had correctly guessed, Mickey thought it would make a great place to begin married life. 'I don't think my life can get any better than this.'

'You so deserve it, Mickey, especially after all I've put you through. I can't believe I was so inconsiderate of your feelings and that I had the audacity to give your dress to Joanna. You must have felt so hurt.'

'Audacity is a good word.' Mickey grinned. 'It's all water under the bridge now. Speaking of water, you've never told me about the riverboat disco. How was it?'

'In my defence, Joanna really did your dress justice. It was perfect and she outshone everyone else on the dancefloor.'

'That's the power of my designs.'

'Yes, it is. I feel like the luckiest man on the planet to have you in my life.'

Mickey had never felt so loved. 'Why don't we throw our going away party on a riverboat disco?'

'That sounds perfect. It can be our engagement party as well.'

Even though he was free to do whatever he wanted, Sam was still not looking forward to breaking the news to Joanna. He wondered if there was any way he could just leave without telling her, but he knew his conscience would get the better of him.

CHAPTER NINE

Joanna had wanted to text Sam. She thought she could innocently ask how he was enjoying his trip, but then she thought better of it. Hadn't she embarrassed herself enough? She couldn't even bring herself to tell Abigail. No, she would contact him one more time, once he was back, and then make her exit dramatically, but gracefully, in a way that he'd never forget. This would be her 'grand romantic gesture' and a final one at that. She felt badly for Abigail, but she was an embarrassment to all and everyone would be better off without her, even her own beloved daughter.

Suzi Quatro's melodic "If You Can't Give Me Love" fittingly played in the background as Joanna began to make her list of things she would need for the last, most important day of her life. Suzi was followed by Charlotte Church belting out "Crazy Chick". She had procrastinated long enough, it was time to get this show on the road. In readiness, she stopped at several different chemists on her way home from work. She wanted to make sure she got the job done. She didn't want to draw attention to herself and bought one large box of Paracetamol from each. She chose the soluble form and wondered if she would be able to taste it in Prosecco. She surprised herself at how matter of factly she approached what was to be a macabre task.

Next, Joanna called the college and, pretending to be a student, asked when Professor McLaughlin would resume teaching his class. She decided to take a gamble on the Saturday following his return. After all, she wouldn't need much of his time.

Her boss at work had noticed a recent change in her disposition and wasn't surprised when she requested a week's holiday. She thought it a good idea.

Her co-workers all assumed that the grim realisation of her impending divorce was finally taking its toll.

She made a hair appointment for the Saturday morning; it was important that she look her best. Now, all that was left to do was confirm a time with Sam and then compose her goodbye letter to Abigail.

Sam felt apprehensive when he saw he had a text from Joanna. Since returning from Italy a few days ago, he had thought about contacting her but decided it best to let the dust settle. He couldn't determine whether it was conscience or cowardice. He was relieved that her message was brief and upbeat. She said she hoped his trip went well and, if he was back, could they facetime Saturday evening? He knew Mickey would be around, but that was probably a good thing. She would see how happy they were together. Joanna anxiously awaited his reply. She was relieved when he set the time for 7:00 pm. His message was concise and businesslike, which served to confirm that she had chosen correctly not to contact him while he was away. He had unknowingly removed all doubt from her mind that if this was setting the stage for their future relationship, she had made the right decision. Hopefully, her plan of action would result in her forever being out of sight but constantly on his mind.

Mickey came and put his arms around Sam's neck and peered over his shoulder at his phone.

'Ooh, a text from JOAnNAh.' Mickey now felt confident enough in his relationship with Sam to over emphasise her name and know that it would come across as humourous, not mean.

'Yes, we're facetiming at 7 on Saturday. It seems as though there's no bad feeling and she's prepared to stay friends. I'd like you to be around.'

'Of course. I'll protect you. I won't let you out of my sight.'

Sam loved this new and playful Mickey. He couldn't imagine his life without him.

It was Joanna's final day at work before her vacation. She was in the lunchroom heating up some soup, even though it was a hot, summer's day.

'Isn't it a bit hot to be eating soup?' remarked Julie from Accounts.

'Probably, but I want to finish everything up.'

Julie assumed Joanna was going away, 'You've picked a nice week for your hols.'

'I guess so.' She took the soup out of the microwave and went back to her desk.

That evening she wrote her most important, distressing and final letter to Abigail, her suicide note. Ironically, she listened to Marc Bolan's "Life's a Gas" as she composed it. Marc had always had a way with words and Joanna believed that he was helping her find the right ones now. She would post it in the morning on her way home from the hairdressers. She had considered sending it as a delayed email but changed her mind. It was kinder for Abigail to receive a note written in her mother's hand. It was late when she had finished and finally got to bed. It seemed that no sooner had she fallen asleep than it was here, the final day of her life.

What began as a typical Saturday morning at the hair salon was a far from typical morning for Joanna. Oblivious, Sue, her stylist, chatted as though they were lifelong friends.

'Are you planning on going away this year?' Sue yanked her hair with the brush and she felt the burning heat of the hairdryer.

'Actually, I am. I'm leaving later today.'

'Somewhere warm and exotic, I hope.'

'I've never been there before, so I don't know. If it's too hot, I'll be in Hell.'

'Don't like the heat, do you? Not me, I love it scorching.'

Joanna didn't encourage further conversation. When done, she tipped Sue well and took her leave. On the way home, she posted her letter to Abigail. It would be delivered on Monday.

The day was passing quickly. Should she eat something or was it easier and quicker to overdose on an empty stomach? She didn't want to throw up and undo all her hard work. In the end she opted for some cheese and crackers. She wanted to remain coherent long enough to speak with Sam.

After she had eaten, Joanna took one last sentimental walk around her house, stopping to reclaim precious memories. She had removed her wedding photos when Mark moved out but there remained photos of family vacations: Abigail at Disneyland wearing her Minnie Mouse ears, Joanna in Montana, crouching and biting her nails, wearing a look of worry worthy of an Oscar as she posed by a sign that read, "Warning! Grizzly bears are active in this area." She paused by the plaque that said, 'I may be old but that's ok, I got to see Marc Bolan in concert!' She hoped Marc Bolan was waiting for her and she would see him soon. She went upstairs and into Abigail's old room. A stuffed rabbit, a bear and a doll with her lips and eyelids coloured purple with a felt tip pen sat guard on the bed. The bookshelf still held well thumbed and well loved copies of Winnie the Pooh, Paddington Bear and Enid Blyton's Naughtiest Girl series that had originally belonged to Joanna. She remembered reading the stories aloud to her daughter at bedtime; she could recite them now, she knew them word for word. Was she losing her resolve? No, this was not the time to reminisce and become maudlin. She hurried into her own bedroom. She looked in the mirror. Sue had done a nice job with her hair. She took the pink sequined dress out of her wardrobe. She hugged it close and then caressed it, remembering the one and only other time she had worn it. How different she had felt then and how stupid of her. Now this evening would be only the second but final time of wearing it. What a waste, but did she mean the dress, her life, or both? Was she having second thoughts? She remembered her last dinner with Sam followed by the grief that had overwhelmed her in the supermarket. No, she couldn't go on. At first, she had lost the art of being happy, now she had also lost the art of living. Her life was unbearable and there was no hope of it changing.

She went downstairs and began to mix her lethal cocktail. She poured a bottle of Prosecco into a pitcher and added the sachets of Paracetamol. She discovered a half empty container of pain killers in her medicine cabinet and also added them to the concoction. They turned the Prosecco an electric blue. She carefully chose her playlist. The first song began, Alcazar's "Crying at the Discotheque". She checked the time. Sam would be calling in less than five minutes. She already felt tipsy from a couple of plain glasses of Prosecco she had drunk earlier. So much for the cheese and crackers.

Her phone rang just as Kylie began to sing, "Spinning Around". It was showtime. Joanna held her phone away from her and twirled so Sam could see that she was wearing the dress.

'Let me call Mickey so he can see you.' She saw the shape of Mickey behind him. 'Doesn't the dress look great on Joanna? Almost as good as it looked on you.'

She couldn't hear Mickey's response but she didn't care. Tonight was all about her.

'What are you drinking?' Sam asked, 'I can see a pitcher of something very blue.'

Joanna thought fast, 'Oh, I'm drinking a Blue Lagoon. Fancied a change from straight up Prosecco or straight down in my case.'

'Don't drink too much or you'll be sorry in the morning.'

Not as sorry as you, Joanna thought, but aloud she said, 'Don't worry, I won't.'

She had planned to keep the conversation going and keep Sam on the phone for as long as possible, but surprisingly she now wanted it to be over. She wanted to be alone with her music and her misery.

Sam did the honours for her, 'Okay, I'll leave you to enjoy the rest of your evening. Looks like you've planned quite a party.'

'Yes, it's the party to end all parties. Ciao.' She didn't even wait for him to reply. She ended the call and stared at the blank screen. Goodbye Sam, that's the last you'll be seeing of me but I'll forever haunt you in your dreams.

CHAPTER TEN

Sam was agitated and so was Mickey, both for the same reason but with different agendas, Mickey's was hidden.

'If you're that worried about Joanna, then why not call the local hospitals and see if she's been admitted?' Now was not the time to enunciate her name.

Sam looked even more concerned, 'Do you really think something bad has happened to her? I just think it strange that she isn't answering her phone.'

Mickey regretted mentioning the hospital, especially when he was desperately trying to conceal firsthand knowledge. Even Sam had noticed a change in him. He wasn't sleeping and appeared to be in a permanent state of dread. The pink dress had become his albatross. Why, oh why, had he capitulated and allowed Sam to give it to Joanna. His act of kindness and generosity had totally backfired and it was all of his own doing. If only he hadn't witnessed Sam facetiming Joanna. It was apparent that she had had too much to drink and he became obsessed with the thought that he must rescue his dress before she vomited and ruined it. His every waking and sleeping moment was now pigmented with memories of that fateful evening like a cancerous growth. It was a malignancy that would not go away.

When Mickey had arrived at Joanna's house, all the lights were still on. He knocked on the door several times but she did not answer. He remembered overhearing her telling Sam where she kept a spare key. It wasn't hard to spot. A small rock, childishly painted in primary colours, was visible by the back door. He lifted it up, and sure enough, there was the key. He let himself in, music was still playing, but there was no sign of Joanna. He called her name, first softly and then more loudly. She didn't answer. He slowly walked up the stairs, he didn't want to alarm her, and then he saw her. The bedroom door was wide open and she was laying on the bed, still wearing his dress. She was out cold. She didn't look at all well and it sounded as though she was having difficulty breathing, as though, at any time, she might stop breathing altogether. He still wanted his dress, but what if she woke up while he was removing it or, even worse, really did take her last breath? He would be accused of attempted rape or murder, or both. He turned and ran down the stairs, but as he went to open the front door, he stopped. What if she did die? How could he live with himself if he didn't at least call an ambulance? He didn't have to stay until it arrived. He went into the living room and made the emergency call from Joanna's landline. He gave her name and address and a brief description of her condition, then he hung up. He let himself out, put the key back under the rock and prayed that no one saw him. Then he drove away as quickly as legally possible, all the while regretting that he had left his abundance of pink sequins and feather trim to an unknown fate.

Mickey's train of thought was interrupted by Sam excitedly answering his phone, Abigail's number was visible on the screen.

'Hi, Abigail? Thank goodness. Is your mum okay? What? No! When did this all happen?'

Mickey did his best to look nonchalant, and then surprised, as Sam continued,'I don't understand. She was fine when we facetimed earlier. She'd obviously had a few drinks, but nothing to be concerned about. No, she didn't tell me she was going anywhere. What was she wearing? Oh, one of Mickey's designs, pink sequined dress that I'd given her. Why do you want to know? Oh, right. She was always going on about how much she loved that dress. It suited her. Listen, I'm so sorry. Let me know when she can have visitors. This is such a shock. Would you like some company, perhaps come here for a home cooked meal? You've gotta keep up your strength for your mum.'

Mickey tried hard not to squirm at the invitation, especially when it became apparent that Abigail had accepted.

'I understand. Let me know what works for you. If there's anything I can do. Great. I'll wait to hear back.'

Even though the conversation had ended, Sam spent a few minutes staring at his phone. Mickey remained silent.

Finally, Sam spoke, 'Joanna's in a bad way at the hospital. She was rushed by ambulance in the early hours of Sunday morning. I can't understand what happened. She seemed fine when we spoke, perhaps a little tipsy but that's all.'

'I'm sure she'll pull through. I heard you invite Abigail over for dinner.' Mickey was already trying to come up with an excuse not to be around.

'Yes. I thought it would be nice for her to have some company and a decent meal. She's spending all her time at the hospital. It's just her, Joanna's too ill to have visitors.'

'Let me know when, and I'll find something else to do, so you two can be alone.'

'Please be here, Mickey. I need your support. I must admit this news has left me pretty shaken.'

Mickey stood up and put his arms around Sam to comfort him. He already knew his fate had been sealed.

* * * * *

She could faintly hear Marc singing "Ride a White Swan". With her eyes still closed, she instinctively went to reach for her lucky swan button that she had left on her bedside table. Her arms were attached to something and she heard a loud metal clang. There were hurried footsteps and she heard the voice of the kindly lady.

'Now, now, no sudden movements. You'll pull out the tubes.' The kindly lady took her hand, 'Your daughter was here a little while ago. It's such a shame she missed seeing you open your eyes. I've told her that you've woken up a few times now.'

How Joanna wanted to see Abigail. She must try and stay awake in case she came back.

The bright light began to give her a headache. She felt disorientated; she knew she couldn't be at home, but she kept forgetting. Please, Abigail, I need you..................and then she faded into the safety of oblivion again.

* * * * *

69

Mickey was upstairs in his workroom. He had heard Abigail arrive but planned on staying put until he couldn't hide any longer. Unfortunately, it happened sooner than he'd hoped.

Sam appeared in the doorway, 'Mickey, would you mind keeping Abigail company while I finish getting dinner? She's come here straight from the hospital and I don't want to leave her alone. She needs a distraction.'

'Is that all I am to you now, a distraction?'

'Yes, and a very pretty one at that.'

Sam introduced them, 'Abigail, this is Mickey, fashion designer to the stars. I briefly told Abigail about your success in Italy.'

Abigail had already formed a picture of Mickey in her head and it was pretty much spot on. He was charismatic and larger than life.

'Hello, Abigail. I'm so sorry about JOAnNAh.'

Abigail was trying to remember where they had met before. She recognised that voice. Sam shot Mickey an embarrassed look. He hadn't meant to pronounce her name that way, it just slipped out, a force of habit. He made a mental note not to do it again.

'So, I finally get to meet the man behind the dress. I have to admit, as lovely as it is, I never expected it to be something my mum would wear.'

Mickey was unsure how to react, 'You'd be surprised. People mistakenly think that if something is shown on the runway, it translates into something they could never wear. Your mum is the perfect example of proving them wrong.'

'I'll have to take your word for it.'

There was an awkward silence while Abigail continued to try and place his voice. Luckily, Sam interrupted the moment to let them know that dinner was ready.

Throughout the evening Abigail asked a lot of questions. 'So how did you two meet?'

'At the college,' Sam replied. 'Mickey was putting on his fashion show and asked me to be the musical director.'

'Have you been together long?'

'Five years.'

Mickey felt as though their relationship was coming under scrutiny. Did Abigail know something and wasn't letting on, or was his guilty conscience getting the better of him? It was a relief when she left to go back to the hospital.

'Mickey, have we met somewhere before? I feel like we have.'

'No, I'm sure you're mistaken.' Mickey felt that he answered too hurriedly.

'Oh well, if you say so, but you're not a person one could easily forget.'

Mickey left Sam to continue his goodbyes and escaped upstairs to his workroom.

'Poor thing. She's so worried about her mum. It's strange that she thinks she's met you before.' Sam walked over and handed Mickey a glass of wine.

'Yes, I can't think where.' Mickey quickly downed his drink.

It was on her way home from the hospital that Abigail remembered. She had to pull the car over to the side of the road to compose herself. That voice, the way he said her mother's name, it was Mickey. He had called the ambulance. But what was he doing at the house? Was he there with Sam? No, Sam had been too worried when he couldn't get hold of her mum. Supposing Mickey was jealous of Joanna's friendship with Sam, so much so that he wanted to do her harm? Yes, that had to be it. She would go to the police with her theory in the morning.

Abigail added a new song to the playlist, Kylie's "Can't Get You Out of My Head". The nurse had told her that Joanna was opening her eyes more frequently and for longer periods of time. She was still very weak, but it was a good sign and she hoped she would be able to say a few words soon. Abigail sat by her mother's side and held her hand. Perhaps today, and with Kylie singing in the background, she would open her eyes while she was there.

* * * * *

She could hear Kylie singing ever so softly. Joanna was on a boat. Sam took her hand and they began to sway to the music.

'Mum, mum, can you hear me?'

She heard Abigail. What was she doing here? She hoped she hadn't come to voice her disapproval. It took a lot of effort to open her eyes, and even more

71

to focus. What had happened to the fairy lights? This bright light bothered her. And where was Sam? Had Abigail chased him away?

Abigail sensed that her mum was disorientated. She squeezed Joanna's hand and spoke softly and slowly.

'Mum, you're in a hospital. You've been very ill but you're getting better. Squeeze my hand if you can hear me.'

Joanna took her time. She had heard her daughter, she had understood what was being said, but none of it rang true. If she wasn't on the boat, then why was she hearing the music. A hospital wouldn't be playing Kylie.

As if reading her mind, Abigail continued, 'You've been unconscious. I've been playing your favourite music in the hope it would help you wake up.'

Joanna slowly began to remember. All those other times when she heard the music, worrying that she was bothering the neighbours, she wasn't at home. She had been in hospital all along.

Joanna squeezed Abigail's hand over and over again. Abigail began to cry.

'Oh mum, you've had us all so worried. I didn't know and I still don't know what happened to you.'

Joanna didn't know either.

* * * * *

Joanna was finally awake, completely. She was propped up on her pillows, taking in her surroundings. The doctor had done his rounds and had asked her some very strange and leading questions. It had all hinged on the results of the toxicology report. No matter what answer she gave, his mind was already made up and he had scheduled an appointment for her to speak with the hospital psychiatrist. This had also not gone well. Yes, she had had feelings of sadness. Who wouldn't if you were getting a divorce after twenty some years of marriage, but there was no way she would do anything to harm herself or leave her daughter without a mother. Whatever had led to her being rushed unconscious to hospital was a complete accident. She was very sorry to have been so careless and to have caused them all so much trouble. She must have mixed painkillers with too much booze, and please don't mention any of this conversation to Abigail.

She was still feeling irritated when Mark appeared in the doorway, flowers in one hand and grapes in the other.

'Don't tell me, you've written out all the lyrics to 'Breaking Up is Hard to Do.'

No sooner were the words out of her mouth than Joanna regretted saying them. If Mark was hurt by her remark, he didn't show it.

'I came as soon as Abbey told me you could have visitors. You've had us all very worried.'

'I'm sorry to have been such a nuisance. It was a complete accident and I feel very foolish.'

There then followed an awkward silence, with both avoiding each other's eyes, even though they desperately needed the cues. They were not certain of the appropriate words to say next and neither wanted to be the first to speak and risk looking the fool. After sharing a lifetime together, their lines had dried up and they needed a prompt. It arrived in the form of Abigail.

'Here dad, give me those, I'll go find a vase. You sit next to mum.'

She deftly took the flowers which were still fresh and lively, unlike Mark, who was fast beginning to wilt.

Joanna was the first to speak, 'How are things with you?'

She was surprised that she even cared, but she did. She also cared that she hadn't had time to brush her hair or put on lipstick.

'Oh, you know, the same old, same old,' but it isn't the same old, thought Mark, because you're not there to share the monotony with me. And I wish you were. He considered his next words carefully.

'Abbey seems to be taking good care of you.'

'Yes, she's been wonderful. I don't know what people do who don't have anyone. I couldn't have managed without her.'

'You would've had me.'

'Don't be silly, Mark. You have your own life now.' Instead of the word life, Joanna almost said Eloise but, at the last minute, couldn't bring herself to say her name.

Mark wanted to tell her that he would always care, but he didn't want to make the situation any more awkward than it already was. Instead, he stood up to leave.

'Bye, Joanna. Have Abbey let me know if you need anything.'

'Bye, Mark. Thanks for coming.'

Abigail was walking back down the corridor with the vase of flowers. 'That was a quick visit, dad.'

'I didn't want to tire her out. She's been through quite an ordeal.'

'I'm sure she was pleased to see you.'

'I hope so. Keep me posted. and thanks for letting me be the first to visit. I'm sure she would have rather seen the boyfriend.'

Before she could think of a kind and appropriate response, Mark kissed her goodbye and left.

Abigail found her mother miles away, deep in thought.

'It was nice of dad to bring you flowers.'

Joanna smiled, 'Yes, it was. Have you heard from Sam?'

CHAPTER ELEVEN

Mickey didn't know whose accusatory looks made him feel more wretched; the Police Officer's or Sam's. It was Mickey's word against whose? There were no witnesses and Joanna didn't remember anything. His interrogation was all down to Joanna's amateur sleuth daughter. All those questions Abigail had asked over dinner. All those pointed looks. Why hadn't she come to him, or Sam, directly? Why did she have to get the Police involved? At least Joanna hadn't died, so he couldn't be accused of murder. Ironically, his actions had probably saved her life. The Police Officer asked Mickey to accompany him to the Station where he would make a formal statement. It seemed as though the whole world was watching as he was escorted outside to the police car. Mickey felt as though all the years of hard work, his lifelong dreams and career, were on the precipice of ruin.

The Detective finished playing Mickey the recording, 'Mr. Harman, can you confirm that it is your voice on the tape and it was you who made the call?'

'Yes, it's me speaking and I made the call.'

'And on the night in question, what was the purpose of your visit to Joanna Stevens' home at 135 Coolgardie Avenue?'

'I wanted to retrieve a dress I had designed that she was wearing.'

'Why did you feel the need to get the dress back?'

'She was obviously drunk and I was concerned that it would be ruined.'

'Did the dress belong to you or Ms. Stevens?'

'Joanna.'

'So why did you behave as though it was your own personal property?'

Mickey had only wanted his dress back. Yes, he was jealous of Sam's friendship with Joanna, but he lived to make Sam happy, and that was why he had let Joanna have the dress in the first place. But when he caught Sam facetiming with Joanna, saw her wearing the dress, it lit a fuse; his emotions went bang like a pent up firework, not a sedate Catherine Wheel, but a for public display only Rocket. Joanna didn't look at all like his dress' muse, Kylie or Sophie, and worse still she was drunk - what if she vomited all over the dress, his dress? He had to get over there and rescue his creation before it was ruined.

Mickey didn't know if he would be able to make the Detective understand, but he had to try. This was his only chance to convince him of his innocence, 'I'm a fashion designer. The clothes I create are my children. I want the best for them and I don't want to see them come to any harm.'

At least the Detective didn't laugh, 'How did Ms. Stevens acquire the dress?'

'Sam gave it to her.'

'Who is Sam?'

'Sam McLaughlin.'

'What is Mr. McLaughlin's relationship to you?'

'We live together.'

'And what is his relationship with Ms. Stevens?'

'They're friends.'

'Were you happy that Mr. McLaughlin gave the dress to Ms. Stevens?'

'Not especially.'

'And why was that?'

Mickey knew things were not going well with this line of questioning. He wished he could bend the truth a little and only admit that he was proud of the dress and wanted to keep it for himself, but he'd been raised never to lie. Instead, he answered, 'I'm not especially fond of Joanna.'

'And why is that?'

'I don't approve of her friendship with Sam.'

'When you say you don't approve, is that because you're jealous?'

Mickey knew that he had dug his own grave, 'A little.' It was probably already a case of too little too late but, finally, a small amount of self-preservation was starting to kick in.

'Did Ms. Stevens let you into her house?'

'No.'

'Why not?'

'She was already unconscious.'

'So how did you gain access?'

'With the spare key. I knew where she kept it.'

The questions were incessant. No, he didn't spike her drink and no, he didn't strike her on the head. He had no idea what events had led to her lying unconscious on her bed. When he saw her, almost lifeless, he had panicked, but he couldn't leave Joanna to her fate; he had called the Paramedics and left.

It was three hours later when he returned home. He found Sam sitting on the sofa, head in hands. He didn't look up.

'I'm sorry, Sam. I just wanted my dress back. I didn't want it ruined.'

'Why didn't you tell me how you felt. I would have gone and got it for you.'

'I know, I'm sorry, but you know how I am about my creations. I wasn't thinking clearly. But it was lucky I did act in haste, because I probably saved Joanna's life.'

Sam still didn't look up. 'Sam, do you love her?' This time he did look up. He looked Mickey straight in the eye, and what felt like the heart.

'No, yes maybe, but not in the way I love you, or at least the person I thought you were.'

Mickey sat down on the sofa next to him. He put his head on Sam's shoulder and began to cry uncontrollably. Sam stroked Mickey's hair. They sat together like that for hours, until Sam's phone rang. It was Abigail. She sounded excited.

'Sam. Mum has regained consciousness and is asking for you. Can you come to the hospital?'

Sam stroked Mickey's head again, and without hesitation said, 'That's great news, Abigail, but I can't be there until tomorrow. Tell Joanna I'll be there in the morning.'

Abigail sounded disappointed, but Sam didn't care. She and her mother had already caused enough trouble, but now was not the time to give Abigail a piece of his mind. Mickey looked up at Sam and gave a weak smile. He knew that he had at least won this battle, although he didn't feel like a winner.

The local press had got hold of the story. When Sam opened the door to go see Joanna in hospital, he was accosted by a reporter.

'Would Mickey Harman like to come out and say a few words about why he was questioned by the police last night?'

'You're wasting your time, he's not here,' Sam lied.

He pushed past the reporter and hurried to his car. He drove around the corner and called Mickey. 'Stay inside until I get back. There's a reporter outside. He's got wind of last night and wants to ask you some questions.'

He heard Mickey sigh heavily, 'I was afraid something like this might happen. What can I do?'

'Stay inside and don't say anything. I'm going to speak to Abigail when I get to the hospital.'

Abigail was waiting at the hospital entrance.

'Is there somewhere we can grab a coffee? I need to speak to you before I see Joanna.'

Sam made it sound important.

'Okay, but I don't like to keep mum waiting. She's so looking forward to seeing you.'

'It won't take long, I promise.'

They found a quiet corner table in the hospital cafe.

Sam wasted no time in getting to the point, 'The police questioned Mickey last night. Seems he called the ambulance for your mum. They wanted to know what he was doing there.'

If Sam had expected Abigail to fake surprise, he was disappointed. 'Yes, I know. I recognised Mickey's voice on the recording after we had dinner that night.'

At least she didn't try to deny her role as instigator, but her perceived complacency annoyed him even more.

'But why, Abigail? Why not come to me first? We've now got the press camped outside our front door.'

'Sam, I want, no, I need to know what happened to my mum. Mickey may have intended to harm her.'

'Mickey may be a lot of things, and hard to comprehend at times, but there isn't a malicious or violent bone in his body.'

'How can you be sure? People live next door to murderers and say they were kind and lovely neighbours.'

'Do you really think that Mickey wanted to harm your mum?'

'Yes, I think it possible. What reason could he have had for being there?'

'He wanted his dress back. Has it occurred to you that he probably saved Joanna's life by calling the ambulance when he did?'

'Has it occurred to you that he might've bottled out at the last minute? What if he was jealous of your relationship with mum? Hell hath no fury like a Mickey scorned.'

Sam didn't want Joanna to have to bear the full brunt of their disagreement, but there was no way he could see her now, given his mood. 'I'm sorry, Abigail, but I'm going to have to leave. Please apologise to Joanna and tell her something came up at the last minute.'

'Sam, please, mum's so looking forward to seeing you. She'll be so disappointed.'

'You should have considered all of the implications before you went to the police. I'm sorry, but I'm too angry right now.'

Sam stormed out of the cafe while Abigail sat stunned. It hadn't occurred to her that she was doing anything wrong by alerting the police. Perhaps Sam was right, she should have first spoken to him, given the situation, but suppose Mickey had intended to cause harm? What if he had felt trapped and turned violent towards her? Now she had to find a way to break the news to Joanna. With a heavy heart, she walked along the corridor to her mother's room.

Sam sat alone in his car. He was too mad to do anything, let alone drive. All of those petty insinuations while Mickey's life and career hung in the balance. He had had no inkling that Abigail felt this way. What if the police thought her assumptions held some merit? The worst was that Sam felt responsible. He was the one who had befriended Joanna and convinced Mickey to give her the dress. How could something so innocent have gone so wrong? He finally calmed down enough to safely drive and was relieved to get home and find the reporter gone. He found Mickey staring at the computer screen.

'Look, it's already online.'

Sam read the headline, "Local Fashion Designer Questioned by Police". It was the lead item.

Mickey continued to read the beginning of the story out loud, "Celebrated Fashion Designer, Mickey Harman, was questioned by police late last night about the emergency call he made from the home of a woman discovered unconscious under suspicious circumstances."

He put his head in his hands, 'I'm ruined. Did you speak to Abigail?'

Sam didn't want to make Mickey feel worse, but he had to speak the truth. 'I did, and you were correct, she recognised your voice and went to the police. I can't believe she doesn't see that she did anything wrong.'

'So she won't lift a finger to help clear my name.' Mickey said it more as a statement of fact than a question.

'Not right now, but I'll have another go and speak to her again.'

'I couldn't bear for this to reach my contacts in Italy. Everything was just starting to happen there for me. You believe I'm innocent, don't you Sam?'

'Of course I do. I never doubted you for a second. If Abigail won't do anything, I'll speak to Joanna. I'll try and get her to issue a statement saying that she is grateful to you for making the call and saving her life.'

'Do you think she would do that?'

'I don't see why not,' but deep down Sam wasn't entirely sure.

Joanna looked at Abigail expectantly, trying to see if Sam was behind her. It was obvious she had gone to great lengths over her appearance. Her hair was styled and she was wearing full make-up. If Abigail hadn't known differently, she would never have guessed that only a few days ago her mum had been gravely ill. The wonders of cosmetics, her mother looked as though she had been photoshopped.

'Where's Sam?'

Abigail had planned to tell Joanna the truth, but the look of disappointment that was already beginning to show on her face made her think better of it. She didn't want her to relapse.

'He sends his apologies but something last minute came up at the college.'

'Did he say when he might be able to stop by?'

'No, he didn't, but I'm sure he won't make you wait too long.'

She shouldn't be building her hopes up but she couldn't help herself. For a brief moment she thought Sam had had a change of heart as Joanna's gaze shifted towards the doorway. She looked surprised.

Two police officers were standing there. 'Ms. Joanna Stevens? May we please have a few words with you, alone?'

There was no time to prepare her mother. Why hadn't she anticipated this. After all, she did work in a law office and this was par for the course.

'Mum, I'll be right outside.'

'But darling, what's happ…..'

Abigail kissed her on the forehead and left before Joanna could finish asking what on earth was going on.

One of the police officers remained standing while the other took the seat next to Joanna's bed.

'We won't keep you long, Ms. Stevens. We realise you've been through quite an ordeal, but there are a few things we would like to know about the night you were brought to the hospital.'

Joanna was sure they had been chosen especially for this assignment; the female detective sitting next to her possessed the manner of a counselor she'd had at school who would always lend a sympathetic ear to her adolescent problems. She was very congenial, a quality that made her very adept at getting a person to open up to her, but why did she want to question her?

The detective leaned in, 'Do you know a Mickey Harman?'

Joanna was even more confused, 'Yes, I do. Why, has something happened to him?'

'No, not yet. How do you know him?'

'He shares a house with a friend of mine.'

'Would you mind telling me the name of the friend?'

'Sam McLaughlin.' Joanna hoped she wasn't getting Sam into any trouble.

'Did you invite Mr. Harman to your home on the night in question?'

'No.'

'Did you let Mr. Harman into your home?'

'No.'

'Do you know how he gained entry?'

'What has Mickey got to do with any of this? He wasn't in my home.'

'Apparently, Ms. Stevens, he was.'

Joanna began to panic. She thought she might be losing her mind and called for Abigail. Abigail rushed back into the room. Her mother had gone from looking photoshopped to photoshocked.

81

'Please stop questioning my mum. Can't you see how distressed you're making her?'

The police detective stood up and nodded to her partner to leave. 'We won't ask any more questions for now, but we may need to come back.'

After they had left, Joanna bombarded Abigail with questions. What did Mickey have to do with her ending up in hospital? Her daughter explained that Mickey had called the ambulance from Joanna's landline.

'So, his quick thinking saved my life.'

'Mum, you're missing the point. Why was he there in the first place? Suppose he went there to hurt you and then panicked.'

'Is this why Sam didn't come and see me today?'

Abigail had to confess, 'Yes, he's really mad with me for calling the police when I realised it was Mickey's voice. He said I should have gone to him first.'

'Maybe you should have.'

'But what if Mickey's dangerous? Suppose he's jealous of your relationship with Sam?'

'What does Sam think?'

'Well, of course he says Mickey's innocent, that he only wanted to save his dress. He saw that you had had too much to drink and was worried you would throw up all over it. I think it's a bit farfetched.'

'I don't. That's probably exactly what happened,' Joanna lied.

She desperately wanted to smooth things over with Sam, but she couldn't help remembering the icy cold look Mickey had given her at the fashion show, nor how uncomfortable he always made her feel. Could he have really wanted to harm her?

CHAPTER TWELVE

Abigail was spending a few hours at the office when Terry called.

'Hi Abigail, how's your mum?'

'She's doing much better, thanks.'

'That's good to hear. Did you recognise the person who called the ambulance?'

'Yes, I did. Thanks for that.'

'Was it the fashion designer, Mickey Harman?'

Abigail instinctively put up her guard in case he was looking for a story. That was the trouble with having a journalist for a friend, you never knew.

'Yes, it was.'

'Thought so. He was questioned by the police as a person of interest. Is there any way you could give me some more details, perhaps even a scoop?'

She'd guessed correctly, he did want a story. 'There isn't anything more I can tell you. Plus, I would prefer if you didn't mention my mum by name if you do write a piece about it. It would only cause her more distress.'

'Understood, but are there any additional details you could give me, no matter how small. What was he doing there?'

Abigail relaxed her guard a little. She was grateful to Terry for sending her the recording and didn't think mentioning the dress would cause any harm. 'He said he was there to get his dress back. Mum was wearing one of his designs, it was a birthday present.'

'Why did he want it back?'

'He thought mum looked a bit tipsy and was concerned that she might ruin it.'

Terry started to laugh, 'Are you serious? What did he think she was going to do?'

'Be sick over it, I guess.'

'For real?'

'Yes, for real. He's very protective of his designs, they're like his children.'

'Do you believe him?'

Abigail hesitated, had she already said too much? 'It's not up to me, it's up to the police to get to the truth. I'm just relieved that my mum is on the mend and will hopefully be home soon.'

'Understood. Thanks, Abigail. I think I can work with what you've told me.'

'Please don't mention any names.'

'Of course I won't. Cheers.'

Abigail had a feeling that she probably shouldn't have said anything at all. If Sam found out, he would want nothing more to do with either her or Joanna ever again.

Mickey came home distraught. 'Everyone at the fashion shoot thinks I'm a joke.'

'Are you sure it's not your imagination?' Sam poured them each a large glass of wine.

'No, there were plenty of snide comments like "make sure you don't puke over the clothes" and it's all because of this. It's all over the internet.'

Sam didn't tell Mickey, but he wasn't entirely surprised. A couple of the faculty had mentioned reading something in the press and asked if it was true. Their reason wasn't to gossip. They were more concerned about Mickey's wellbeing and how he was holding up.

Mickey turned his laptop around so Sam could see what he was talking about. 'It's that local reporter again. He's really got it in for me.'

Terry had used the information given to him by Abigail and written another story.

'Where would he have got this from? The police wouldn't have said anything, the investigation is still ongoing.'

'I don't kn…..' Mickey paused mid-sentence.

They both looked at one another, 'Abigail.'

'I'm going to put an end to this right now.' Sam grabbed his car keys.

'Where are you going? To see Abigail?'

'No, I'm not wasting my breath on her. I'm going to speak to Joanna.'

The nurse tried to block his way but Sam would not be stopped. 'Sir, visiting hours are over.'

'This is very important. Besides, Ms. Stevens will want to see me. You can ask her if you want.'

'Yes, I do want. Please wait here.'

The nurse walked briskly along the corridor and rounded the corner into Joanna's room. She returned almost immediately and nodded for Sam to follow her, 'I can't let you stay too long. You shouldn't be here in the first place, it's late and she needs her rest. I'll be back in fifteen minutes.' She gave him a disapproving look.

Joanna wished she'd had time to fix her hair and put on some make up, but she was thrilled that Sam had had a change of heart and come back to see her. This was her chance to smooth things over, although the expression on his face was not very encouraging.

'Joanna, as I don't have much time I'll come straight to the point. Your daughter appears to have launched a vendetta against Mickey.'

'Don't be silly. She's just being overly protective of me.'

Sam was becoming exasperated. 'I don't think either you or Abigail realise all the harm you are causing with this witch hunt.'

Joanna had never seen him so angry. 'Sam, I'm sorry, I had no idea. Is there something I can do?'

'You bet. For one you can tell that nosy reporter to back off and Abigail can quit feeding him information. People like him are the scum of the earth. Secondly, please tell the police that Mickey was only there to get the dress back. He had nothing to do with whatever landed you here in hospital.'

'I'm sure Abigail didn't speak to any reporter, but I'll ask her. As for the police, how can I be certain that Mickey didn't try to hurt me? The police are going to have to continue their investigation until they are able to determine what happened.'

'So, Abigail's got you believing her malicious lies now. How can you not believe Mickey?'

'What reason do I have to believe him? He's never liked me.'

'But that doesn't mean he'd hurt you. There's lots of people I don't like but I would never do them any harm.'

Sam knew he was raising his voice. The nurse came running into the room accompanied by a doctor.

'Sir, you'll have to leave now. You'll upset the patient.'

'Joanna, I'm begging you. Please give what I said some serious thought.'

On his way out of the door, Sam turned around and gave her a pleading look that swiftly turned to one of anger. She could feel the heat emanating from his blue eyes, they were on fire.

The nurse looked concerned and took her temperature. 'Are you okay? It sounded like he was intimidating you.'

'No, everything's fine. We just had a slight disagreement.'

But Joanna knew that everything wasn't fine. It was far from it.

While Sam was visiting Joanna, Mickey called Giana. He wanted her to hear his version of events rather than get them from the internet. Giana was a sympathetic ear and thought Joanna most ungrateful after he had given her the bellissima dress. She asked if he felt up to visiting her. Mickey would have loved to have got on a plane right there and then, but he thought the police would interpret this as an act of guilt and say he had fled the country. Giana was disappointed, but understood, and said she would make sure that all her contacts knew the true story if they happened to find out.

'By the way, I completely get how you felt about that dress. I have the same emotions about my songs. They are my creations, from my heart.'

'Thanks, G. I knew you'd understand.'

When Sam arrived home, Mickey could tell by his demeanour that things hadn't gone well.

'Joanna believes all of Abigail's lies. I couldn't reason with her. I'm sorry. This is all my fault. I should never have given her the dress in the first place.'

Mickey got up and stood behind Sam who had sat down on the sofa. He began to rub Sam's already defeated and tense shoulders.

'Please don't blame yourself. I'm the one who went over there in a fit of panic. If anyone's to blame, it's Abigail and the way she likes to go behind our backs to stir up trouble. At least Giana is on our side.'

'Did you speak to her?'

'Yes, she totally gets this and understands. Hopefully she'll be able to save my career in Italy. She invited me over for a visit, but I didn't want the police to think I was fleeing the country.'

'Mickey, don't! Now you're making yourself sound like a criminal.'

'For all intent and purposes, I am. At least they didn't seize my passport.'

Sam managed a weak smile, 'Okay, which one of us is Bonnie and which one is Clyde?'

'I'm Bonnie of course.' Mickey replied without hesitation.

Then right on cue, they both said in unison,' Only prettier.'

Even the seriousness of the moment could not prevent them from both bursting out laughing.

CHAPTER THIRTEEN

It was late to still be at work, even for Rosemary. It used to be the two of them. The interconnecting doors to their individual offices permanently open, unless meeting with clients, so they could spar back and forth. But that had all ended three years ago when her husband's heart attack had surprised them both and left her the sole practitioner at the law firm of Elphick & Elphick. Her husband had been her partner in both her personal and professional life, and his sudden departure had left a huge void, one that she chose to fill with work.

Rosemary Elphick was a well-respected attorney. She specialised in family law and made it a priority to always fight for what was in the best interest of the child. She had entered the legal profession a little later than intended. Always bright and studious at school, she chose to rebel during her final year and, as a consequence, didn't pass the necessary exams to earn her the expected place at University. She remained off the rails for quite some time before life brought her to a sudden and screeching halt. Before being derailed, she had intended to study law, so she turned her life around and began studying again. She was certain that she wanted a profession that allowed her to help people, especially young people. Family law was the perfect fit and something at which she excelled. She was neither harsh nor judgemental, and possessed excellent problem solving skills as well as a more than generous helping of empathy. "Never judge another unless you have walked in their shoes" was one of her favourite quotes.

Rosemary put the file she was working on in her briefcase and focused her attention on the story she had been reading earlier. She smiled at the photo they had used. He looked so much like her, and those same curls. She wondered if he had always embraced them or, like her, spent the adolescent years using all manner of potions in the elusive hope of a sleek and straight transformation. She felt sure he was happy with his appearance. He had inherited the best of genes from them both; in fact, he was more pretty than handsome. Now he needed both her personal and professional support and assistance, and she felt as though she had been waiting for this moment all of her adult life; she could finally do something for him. It was time.

Before she left, and as she had done every evening for the past three years, Rosemary walked into the adjacent empty office to say goodnight. She blew a kiss at the empty maroon Chesterfield chair. She ran her fingers along the edge of the heavy mahogany desk which remained bare. It was almost a caress. She remembered when she couldn't see the surface for paper, a bottle of cognac and a box of Cuban cigars. She had always sat and joined him, exchanging lighthearted banter as they discussed the matters of the day and relaxed before heading home.

She expected he would have tried to talk her out of it, 'But I'm doing this by myself, for myself,' she whispered.

She was sure she heard the chair creak as he signaled that he understood.

Rosemary let herself into the empty house which always felt colder these days. She went straight to her bedroom and removed a wooden box from the top shelf of her closet. The box, monogrammed, had once housed an assortment of chalks, pencils and paints from the days when she enjoyed nothing more than to relax with a sketchbook or easel. She had been a rather good artist and had even sold a few watercolour scenes of Italy, mainly painted from memory when she had visited as a student. Now the box no longer contained these creative implements of her youth, but her most treasured possessions: letters and photos going back over thirty years. On the very top was a photo taken on his tenth birthday that reflected an inexplicable change. His tenth birthday had always stuck in her mind because she had asked if they would buy him an art set, similar to the one she had once owned. They were always more than considerate of her feelings, considering the circumstance, and had done as she had requested, hence the photo. There he stood by his birthday cake, proudly holding the wooden case, but something in his expression had changed. Overnight, his composure had gone from self-assured to self-conscious and she could never understand the reason why. She began to plan what she was going to say during her visit tomorrow. It was going to take a lot of restraint not to introduce herself, but he didn't deserve that. If he chose to find her, then that would be different. It had to be on his terms. No, her appointment was going to be with one Ms. Joanna Stevens.

She had done her homework. LinkedIn had turned up no results, but she had found Joanna's profile on Facebook. Her cover photo was of Marc Bolan and his band, T. Rex, who Rosemary immediately recognized because she was familiar with their hit, "Telegram Sam", with its reference to corkscrew hair. She wondered if he was also familiar with the song for the very same reason, but suspected that it was probably a bit before his time. She clicked on the profile photo and it enlarged to show Joanna wearing what had to be 'the dress'. After the way it had been described, Rosemary was surprised to discover that it quite suited her. There were other photos and snippets of information that offered some additional insight: she had an adult daughter, she was recently separated, and her favourite quote was from Oliver Goldsmith's play 'She Stoops to Conquer' – "Women and music should never be dated". Rosemary had already devised her strategy. She would not approach Joanna as a lawyer, but instead appeal to her sensibilities as a mother.

'But darling, please stop and listen to me. I have to agree with Sam on this one. You should never have spoken to that reporter.'

'Mum, it's nothing he wouldn't have found out for himself.'

Joanna sighed into the phone. Her daughter could sometimes be so stubborn. Abigail, on the other hand, was certain her mother's opinion was swayed because it involved Sam.

'Promise me you will now leave all of this to the police. No more meddling because….'

Her voice trailed off because someone had entered the room, a woman she didn't recognize, although she did look slightly familiar. 'Abigail, I have to go. Someone's here. We'll talk more about this later.'

'Is it Sam?', but Joanna had hung up before Abigail got her answer.

'Hello, Joanna. I do hope you will forgive me for arriving unannounced, but the nurse said it would be alright, as long as I don't stay too long. I'm glad to see that you're feeling better.' Rosemary handed Joanna her business card.

'Rosemary Elphick, Counselor at Law,' Joanna read aloud, 'Are you here about the investigation?'

'Yes, but not in the way you think.'

Joanna still couldn't place the face, but she was sure they had met before. There was something about her hair and eyes.

'I'm Mickey Harman's mother.'

So that was the reason for the resemblance. Joanna was taken by surprise, 'Oh, I had no idea. Did he ask you to come and see me?'

'No, Mickey doesn't know I'm here and I'd rather we kept it that way.'

'Then why are you here?'

'I'm here to appeal to you as a mother, not a lawyer. I admit that my son used poor judgement on the night in question, but he had no intention of harming you. We have all acted impulsively at times, and not thought through the possible consequences of our actions. Mickey's only motive was to retrieve his dress and prevent it from being ruined. In one way it was unfortunate because you were unconscious when he arrived, but in another way it was also a fortunate turn of events because he was able to call an ambulance and get you the medical attention you needed.'

Joanna was not entirely convinced, 'How can you be so sure that Mickey was not out to hurt me?'

'Because I know my son, in the same way you know your daughter. Mickey isn't perfect, none of us are, but there is no way he would set out to hurt anyone. His sole motivation that night was to save his dress. Instead, he saved your life.'

Joanna was convinced that not many could surpass Rosemary in the courtroom, but she was still prepared to put up a fight. 'I think we should leave the final conclusion to the police.'

Rosemary leaned in for the kill and began her closing argument, 'Joanna, we can't always protect our children, but we can always want what's best for them. Mickey has a fine career ahead of him and the stories in the press have already begun to jeopardise it. Even if his intentions had been otherwise, and I know this not to be the case, in the end he did what was right. He got you the help that probably saved your life. For that alone he deserves to be able to put all of this behind him. We all deserve a second chance.'

Boy, she was good. 'So, what do you want from me?' Joanna already knew the answer.

'I want you to tell the police that this was all a misunderstanding and you are not going to press charges. Then I want you to contact the press and put out a statement saying the same but also adding that you are very grateful to Mickey for his swift action in saving your life.'

'I'm not sure.'

'Joanna, wouldn't you do the same for your daughter? I'm asking this of you, mother to mother. It's the right thing to do. In fact, it's the only thing to do.'

Joanna didn't need any more persuading but she needed to speak to Abigail first. 'Let me think about it.'

'Please don't take too long. My son's career and future are at stake. I hope you will make the right decision but, remember, please don't tell anyone I was here. I don't want to cause Mickey further embarrassment. He's already been through enough.'

And with that, Rosemary left. She had just won the most important case of her life.

Abigail had just heard back from the police. Their investigation was complete and there wasn't enough evidence to support any charges against Mickey other than trespassing. It was entirely up to Abigail and Joanna to decide if they wanted to take things further. When Abigail arrived at the hospital, she found Joanna deep in thought.

'Hi mum, a penny for them.'

'Oh, hi honey.'

'So, who was your surprise visitor?'

'Mickey's mother.' She handed Abigail the business card. She knew Rosemary had asked her to not tell anyone but she didn't see the harm in telling Abigail.

'Wow, I'm impressed. Mickey's mother is Rosemary Elphick? She's my hero. I studied one of her cases at law school. What's she like?'

'She wasn't here for very long. She asked me to drop all charges.'

'Of course she did. The police contacted me earlier. They said the only charge we could possibly pursue is one for trespassing.'

'She also asked me to issue a statement to the press saying that it was all a misunderstanding and that I am grateful to Mickey for saving my life.'

'Is that how you feel?'

'There's no denying that if he hadn't called the ambulance, I might not be here.'

'So, what do you want to do?'

'I'm going to drop the charge and make a statement to the press. Will you get in touch with your journalist friend for me?'

'As long as you're completely sure about this?'

Rosemary's parting words still rang in Joanna's head, 'Yes, it's the right thing to do. In fact, it's the only thing to do.'

Abigail stood up to leave, 'I'll call Terry now at the newspaper and ask him to stop by and speak to you. I'll also let the police know.'

'Thanks, and one last thing, will you please tell Sam?'

On her way home from seeing Joanna, Rosemary stopped by her office. She went directly to the chair across from the desk where he used to sit and opened a bottle of wine for one that she had purchased on the way.

'Cheers! You would've been very proud of me. No histrionics, just the facts, presented in a motherly fashion.' She waited to sense his response. 'Yes, I know what you're thinking and you're probably right. Even though I asked her to keep my visit a secret, she probably won't.' He could read her so well. 'Okay, I confess, I secretly hope he does find out and comes to see me. There, are you satisfied now?'

She went around to his side of the desk. She stood behind his beloved Chesterfield chair and bent down and kissed the air at the point where the top of his head used to reach. 'I love and miss you so very much. Please don't ever completely leave me.'

Abigail decided to text Sam. There was so much bad feeling between them that he probably wouldn't answer her call anyway.

Thought you'd want to know that mum's not pressing charges. She's also going to issue a statement to the press saying that it was all a misunderstanding and she is grateful to Mickey for calling the ambulance and saving her life.

Sam replied immediately.

What changed her mind?

A visit from Mickey's mum.

Mickey's mum???

Sam couldn't believe what he was reading.

Yes, she convinced my mum that Mickey was telling the truth about only wanting to save his dress. I didn't know his mum was Rosemary Elphick.

Who's Rosemary Elphick?

I thought you would know. Haven't you met her? She's a very well-respected lawyer.

No, I haven't met her. Please thank Joanna for her change of heart and thanks for letting me know. I'll go tell Mickey now.

Before Sam spoke to Mickey, he googled Rosemary Elphick. She did indeed have a stellar reputation as a lawyer. She also bore an uncanny resemblance to Mickey. There was no doubt in Sam's mind that they were related.

Mickey was in his workroom. The frustration was apparent in his voice, 'I'm trying to design a dress for Giana to wear at an awards show but nothing will come. I can't concentrate with all the stress of what's happened.'

'Calm down, I have good news. This nightmare is about to come to an end. Joanna is dropping all charges and, more importantly, she's making a statement to the press that this was all a misunderstanding and she is grateful to you for saving her life.'

'How do you know? Are you sure?'

'Absolutely. Abigail just texted me.' Sam could tell that Mickey still had his doubts.

'But what changed her mind?'

'It's not a what but a who. This is going to shock you, but Joanna had a visit from your mother.'

'I don't understand. Mum doesn't go on the internet much and I haven't told her. I'd be very surprised if she knew about this yet, unless, unless, oh no,' Mickey's voice trailed off and he put his head in his hands, 'don't tell me the story's on TV?'

'Calm down. It's not that at all and it's not the mother you're thinking of.'

'Sam, you're making no sense at all.'

'Mickey, Joanna had a visit from your birth mother.'

Mickey just stared at Sam as though he had lost his mind. Sam grabbed his laptop and brought up the website for Elphick & Elphick. He put the evidence in front of Mickey.

'This is your mother, Rosemary Elphick. She's a lawyer. Just look at her. There's no denying you're related.'

Mickey just sat and stared at the screen for a very long time. He ran his hands through his hair and then looked from the screen, back up at Sam, and back at the screen again.

In a very quiet voice he said, 'Yes, but I'm prettier.'

Joanna was true to her word. The next day her statement was in the press. What a difference a headline made, "Local Fashion Designer a Hero for Saving Woman's Life." Underneath a photo taken of Joanna sitting up in her hospital bed was the quote, "It was all a huge misunderstanding and I will forever be grateful to Mickey Harman for his swift action." Sam thanked Joanna by text. She was disappointed, she had hoped he would visit her in person. She had to find a way to make things right between them again.

Rosemary also read the words that accompanied Joanna's photo. She went over to the window and looked down at the street below. 'How long do you think I'll have to wait?' She turned and fixed her gaze on his empty chair, 'I know, you don't want me to get my hopes up, but he will come. I know my own son.'

CHAPTER FOURTEEN

Mickey decided to spend a few days with Giana in Italy and go over his ideas for what she should wear to present the awards show. Now with his name cleared and reputation still intact, he could put the events of the past few weeks behind him and get back to doing what he loved the most. The ideas flowed and his creativity knew no bounds. This time he was unstoppable. Giana loved his emerald green sequined midriff top and shorts, complete with a long flowing train. She also gave him the news that there was interest from a large fashion house in Milan who were considering giving him his own label. How did The House of Harman sound? Mickey was beside himself and couldn't wait to tell Sam. He called him later that evening.

'If this all goes ahead, we really should finalise our plans and move here.'

Sam had already been thinking along the same lines. They both deserved a new start.

'I certainly wouldn't be opposed. I'll reach out to that guy I met at the record company and see if his offer still stands.'

'Would you? That would be great. Ciao baby! Love you.'

'Love you too.'

While Mickey was away, Sam decided to pay Joanna another visit in hospital and thank her for having a change of heart. He hoped he wouldn't run into Abigail, but if he did, he wouldn't let her presence deter him. He'd say what he'd come to say and leave.

Joanna had her earbuds in and was listening to "Altered Images". She didn't hear Sam approach. When she looked up and saw him, she instinctively reached for her mirror. She wasn't happy with what she saw. She still looked like she'd been through the wringer. Why hadn't she bothered with her make-up? Up until a few days ago, she had been meticulously applying foundation, blush, mascara and lipstick in the hope that Sam might pay her a visit. When he didn't show, she finally convinced herself that the effort was futile. Now she was having regrets. She put the mirror down, deflated.

'Sorry I didn't let you know I was coming. I hope you're feeling up to visitors.' Sam gave her a chaste kiss on the cheek.

Did she really look that bad? 'It's fine. I'm glad to see you.'

'Sorry it's taken me a while but I wanted to personally come and thank you for seeing sense and clearing Mickey's name.'

So now she was the one seeing sense. He made it sound as though she had been in the wrong all along.

Unaware of her feelings, Sam continued, 'Abigail told me that Mickey's birth mother came to see you.'

She remembered that Rosemary had not wanted anyone to know about her visit. She probably shouldn't have mentioned it even to Abigail.

'Yes, but she wanted to keep it just between the two of us. She was very convincing. Did you say birth mother?'

It had innocently slipped out, but Sam felt guilty that he had probably said too much. 'Yes, Mickey's adopted.' It was too late now.

'I had no idea. Are they close?'

He had no choice but to reply, 'Mickey's never met her.'

'So that's probably why she wanted to keep her visit a secret. It's obvious that she cares deeply for him. How sad that they've never met.'

Sam was feeling awkward. 'I'd rather this conversation didn't go any further.'

'Of course not. How's Mickey?'

'He's back in Italy. Things are going really well for him career wise,' Sam attempted to steer the conversation in another direction.

'Do you think he might eventually move there?' Joanna didn't really care where Mickey made his home, but she was concerned about whether Sam would follow.

'He's mentioned it once or twice.' Sam tried to make it sound casual. When they did finally make the move, he would wait until the very last minute to tell Joanna.

They both sat in silence. Joanna didn't want to talk anymore about Mickey and Sam didn't think they had anymore left to say.

After what seemed longer than a few minutes, he stood up to leave. 'Bye, Joanna. Hope you'll feel well enough to go home soon.'

Once he had disappeared from view, she picked up her mirror again. She was still the same person whose company and friendship Sam had previously enjoyed so much. She recalled the Eurovision party and the riverboat disco for her birthday. What had changed? Perhaps she needed a new playlist.

On the last evening of his trip, Mickey told Giana that he had found his birth mother.

'That's incredible. What's she like?'

'I haven't met her. All I know is her name and that she's a lawyer. Look.'

Mickey pulled up the Elphick & Elphick website on his phone.

'So how did you find her?'

'She went to see Joanna in hospital. She's the one who convinced her to drop the charges.'

'So she didn't get in touch with you first?'

'No. Abigail told Sam about her visit. She hasn't been in touch with me at all.'

'Are you going to contact her?'

'I'm not sure. I want to, but what if she doesn't want to see me? Why would she go and see Joanna and not me?'

'Hmmm, probably because she wanted you to be the one to contact her first. She wants it to be on your terms. I think it's wonderful that she went to those lengths to help you when she knew you were in trouble.'

'Me too. I'd like to be able to say thank you in person.'

'Then why don't you?'

'I'm not sure. Something's holding me back. At first, I was so thrilled to discover that she knew about me and wanted to help me. But now I'm not so sure. Everything's so perfect at the moment. I don't want to do anything to burst my bubble and spoil things.'

'Is that what you think could happen?'

'I worry that I might be disappointed if we meet face to face. Supposing it's awkward?'

'When the time's right, you'll know what to do.'

'Thanks, G. You always know the right things to say. If I wasn't gay, I'd marry you.'

'That's the nicest thing anyone has ever said to me. The ultimate compliment.' Giana grinned. She had a smile big enough to light up not just a room, but a building, and a skyscraper at that.

They walked back to the hotel, arm in arm. To an outsider, they appeared the perfect couple.

'So how did your Zoom meeting go?'

'Practically signed, sealed and delivered.'

Mickey had been home less than a week and had just had an official meeting with the head designer at the Milan fashion house. He was going to design for his own fashion label and be based in Rome so he could still work closely with Giana. They had already discussed the launch and Giana was going to feature in the ad campaign.

'I have good news, too. I reached out to my contact at Giana's record label, they still have an opening and I just have to let them know when I can start.' Sam knew that the switch in career and leaving behind his students and colleagues would be a wrench, but both he and Mickey needed a fresh start. Italy had worked its magic before and there was no reason to think that it couldn't happen again. 'Changing the subject. Have you been in touch with Rosemary?'

Sam didn't want anything to jeopardise the move and he thought that Mickey's mother had the potential to be a loose end that might unravel at any given moment.

'Not yet, I've been thinking about it. But you know what, I've just decided, I'm going to see her right now.'

Mickey first drove slowly past the building. What little he knew of Rosemary, and given her reputation, he envisioned one of the newer office blocks, but this was much older, almost dilapidated. She would probably defend it as having character. He wondered if she had a maternal sixth sense and knew that he was nearby? Was she standing at one of the windows, inexplicably looking down on the street below, guided by his presence? This was too much romanticising. He decided to park in one of the side streets, compose himself and prepare what he was going to say. Supposing she wasn't there? She might be in court. Should he call the number on the website to check? Was the element of surprise such a good idea, although she was probably expecting him at some point? He was overthinking and that, in itself, gave him his answer. There was no more doubt. He started the car again and drove straight home.

Sam was surprised to see Mickey home so early. He hoped it hadn't all gone wrong, but Mickey didn't seem upset.

'So, how did it go?'

'I changed my mind. I didn't go in.'

'What? How come?'

'I ended up listening to my gut, not my heart.'

'I don't understand.'

'It's all about the timing and now isn't the right time. With my career and us moving to Italy, everything is falling into place. My mum stepping in when I most needed her is the icing on the cake, but I'm wary of doing something that could tip the balance and spoil it all. I have this feeling that it could change everything and not in a good way. It's best that I leave it alone for now.'

'Well, it sounds as though you've thoroughly thought this through and you're coming from a good place.'

'Believe me, I am.'

'Speaking of good places, I've decided to rent out this house. There are plenty of interested faculty at college, and some students, too. I shouldn't be short on tenants.'

'That sounds great, and Giana can get us an apartment in her building until we find a place to live for the long term.'

'Then we're all set, we just have to say our goodbyes.'

Mickey knew Sam meant Joanna.

CHAPTER FIFTEEN

Everything looked just the same. Why would she have expected her cottage to look any different? She'd only been in the hospital for three weeks but she felt like a stranger in her own home. She had hoped there might be flowers or a card from Sam. She talked herself out of her disappointment by reminding herself that he probably didn't know she was coming home today. She was certain Abigail wouldn't have thought to tell him.

'I've kept up the dusting and vacuuming,' Abigail called from the kitchen, 'Shall I make us both a cup of tea?'

'Don't bother. I'll be fine now. You get back to your own life. I've already taken up too much of your time. Thank you for all you've done.'

'Well don't overdo and just holler if you need me to do anything.'

'You've done more than enough. I don't know what I would do without you.'

Joanna watched Abigail get in her car. She blew her a kiss and closed the door. She was very proud of the self-assured woman her daughter had become but she also worried that the example she and Mark had set at the end of their marriage had made Abigail wary of any future romantic involvement. She had so much to give and Joanna worried that she might be lonely. She didn't seem to do anything outside of work. She knew she was ambitious, but she needed to also have fun. She hoped she wasn't crying at the discotheque. She would have to find a good time to talk to her and find out how she really felt.

Something had been playing on her mind. She went upstairs to her bedroom and let out a sigh of relief. It was still there. Lying on her bedside table was her lucky swan button. She picked it up and held it to her lips. Like so many times before, she closed her eyes and made a wish.

When Abigail got home, she called Mark. 'Hi dad, just letting you know that mum is home.'

'How does she seem?'

'Remarkably well, considering how worried we all were.'

'Do you think she should be left alone?'

'Yes, she'll be fine. She didn't even want me to stay for a cup of tea.'

'I'll give it a couple of days and then call her. Perhaps offer to get her some shopping.'

'Dad, you don't need an excuse to see her.'

'I know, but it still feels kind of awkward.'

'I'm sure she'll be happy to hear from you.'

Abigail knew he wondered why Sam wasn't being of more help, but she honestly didn't know how to explain. It was better for everyone to be left in the dark for the time being.

Mark was as good as his word. Joanna had only been home a few days when he stopped by. The knock at the door took her by surprise. She knew it couldn't be Abigail because she had only just spoken to her on the phone. She began to get butterflies, supposing it was Sam? Yes, that's who it must be. With excited anticipation, she hurriedly opened the door only to see Mark standing there. The look on her face must have said it all because he awkwardly asked if this was a good time. She noticed a French baguette sticking out of one of the bags he was holding and realised she was hungry.

'No, you're fine. Come on in.'

Mark went directly to the kitchen. 'I'll put these away for you. I thought you could probably do with stocking up on a few basics.'

'Yes, you're right. Thank you. I am beginning to get my appetite back.'

She could hear him opening and closing the doors to her cupboards and fridge.

'Actually, Mark, I'm glad you stopped by because there's something I've been wanting to talk to you about. It's to do with our relationship and………'

Now it was his turn to get his hopes up. He'd been wanting to talk to her about the possibility of their getting back together.

Before she could finish, Mark appeared in the room, 'And? Go on.'

'I was going to say and the effect it's having on Abbey.'

He tried not to let his disappointment show as Joanna continued, 'She doesn't seem to have any social life and I wonder if we've put her off going out there and meeting someone.'

'Oh, I don't think we have anything to do with it. She's still young and focused on her career. The time will come when she's ready. Anyway, when we were together, I think we set a pretty good example, for the most part.'

'Maybe. I'm just concerned. I want her to be happy.'

'And she is happy. Let her live her own life. She's got a good head on her shoulders. We've been very lucky. She's never given us any trouble.'

They began to smile as they both remembered at the same time, 'Except for Mrs. Bell Bottoms!'

Joanna got a fit of the giggles. 'I can still see us at the Parent Teacher Night. How many times did we call her that?'

'Four or Five,' Mark was laughing too. 'I can still see your face when you read Abbey's report card after and her teacher had signed it Beryl Bottoms.'

'I should have guessed that Mrs. Bell Bottoms wasn't her real name. I was mortified.'

They had shared so much and it felt good to laugh. Mark wondered if he should say what was really on his mind, but Joanna had turned to check her phone. Perhaps it was a text from the new boyfriend.

'Well, I'd better be on my way.'

'Are you sure?'

'Yes, I have some work to catch up on. Don't worry about Abbey. I'm sure she's fine. I'll see myself out.'

Joanna was surprised at how much she had enjoyed Mark's visit. She wished he could have stayed longer.

Joanna opened her closet and took out the dress. What had once been a vibrant source of delight and optimism had now faded into a sordid reminder of all that had gone wrong. She didn't want it anymore, but how to dispose of something that was still quite unique and lovely? And then the idea came to her, she would give it to Rosemary. She was sure she would love to have one of her son's designs. She checked that she still had Rosemary's business card with her address. She would get the dress professionally cleaned right away and send it to her.

Although Joanna had intended the gift of the dress to be a gesture of kindness, Rosemary interpreted it otherwise. She read the note that Joanna had enclosed.

Dear Rosemary,
I thought you would want to have this proof of your son's incredible talent.
Wear it in joy and wear it in love.
Joanna

Rosemary stood in front of his desk and held the dress up to her. She dramatically and scornfully made a point of blowing the feathers away from her face.

'So, what do you make of this? Should I wear it?'

She began to laugh uncontrollably and then she began to weep. She threw the dress to the floor.

'What reason do I have? What occasion? I've lost my husband and now I've lost my son. How did I manage to be so careless?'

As she drove home along the High Street, Rosemary noticed some black plastic sacks sitting on the pavement outside a charity shop. She parked her car, grabbed the bag containing the dress and added it to the pile of donations. Rosemary continued on her way and never once looked back.

Abigail fancied a change. She had always admired Rosemary Elphick and hoped she might be in need of the help of a paralegal. The offices of Elphick & Elphick were nothing like she'd imagined. They were listed as being on the third floor of an old building that had seen better days. She didn't trust the lift and took the stairs. The bottom steps were littered with stray leaves and a discarded empty crisp packet. Rosemary Elphick needed to have strict words with the property management company. The third floor was deserted and almost spooky. The lettering on the door, once gold, was faded and obliterated in places, like chipped nail polish. Abigail was beginning to have a change of heart. She tried the door and, as she expected from all outward appearances, it was locked. She found a small window halfway along the corridor and peeked in. The office was devoid of any furniture. In fact, it was completely empty. It was obvious that Elphick & Elphick had moved on.

'You just missed her.'

Abigail almost jumped out of her skin. She turned to see who had spoken. It was the janitor.

'I beg your pardon?'

'Mrs. Elphick. She was just here having one last look around. Known her for years, I have, and her husband before he passed. Never thought she'd ever give up the firm. Just goes to show.'

'So she's no longer practicing law?'

'No, sorry, I hope you weren't counting on her to help you. She was quite something. Said it was time for her to retire.'

'I hadn't realised.'

'She said something about moving to Italy to paint.'

'Sounds nice and relaxing.'

'Yes, the stress of being a lawyer probably got to her in the end.'

'You're probably right. Thank you for the information.'

'Can I give her a message? I'll probably see her here again before she goes abroad.'

'No, thank you. You've already been more than helpful. I'll just have to find myself another lawyer.'

Abigail wondered what had caused Rosemary to quit her profession so suddenly. She had struck her as the type of person who thrived on adrenalin and performed best under stress. By no means was she ready to retire, plus it was a devastating loss to the legal community. For once, and totally out of character, Abigail made up her mind to practice restraint and let it go. It was none of her business.

105

CHAPTER SIXTEEN

Joanna knew she had to convalesce but she found herself with too much time on her hands. Time that she knew she was using unproductively by repeatedly checking her phone for a text from Sam. Inexplicably, something stopped her from making the first move and reaching out to him. Too much overthinking had given her another one of her 'heads'. The hospital had sent her home with some very strong and potent pills. She had taken them on a couple of previous occasions, but they really knocked her out. She decided to see if Paracetamol would do the trick instead. She was surprised to find several opened empty boxes sitting in her bathroom cabinet. Each had once contained large quantities of the drug. When and why had she bought so many and, even more worrying, why were the boxes now sitting empty? Had she been having bad headaches prior to whatever landed her in hospital? Unless...............no, her mind was playing tricks. She wouldn't, she couldn't..... She had to lie down, she felt as though a thunderstorm was happening inside her head with the lightning running full throttle behind her eyes. As she lay on the bed, hoping the pain would eventually subside on its own, Joanna was transported back to when she was lying here all those weeks ago wearing the pink sequined dress. It was almost an out of body experience and she felt as though she was going mad. Try as she might, and no matter how hard she tried to summon little nuggets of memory, she repeatedly drew a blank. Her headache grew worse and she had to give in and take one of the pills prescribed by the hospital. When she awoke, no longer in pain, she couldn't even remember how she had got upstairs and into her bed. With all of these memory lapses, what vital pieces of information was she missing? She was sure they must have something to do with Sam.

Joanna decided she needed fresh air and exercise, and what better way than to take a daily walk in the park where she and Sam had met for lunch all those weeks ago before everything went wrong. Why, she might even run into him. By the third day, Joanna began to feel like a stalker but she couldn't help herself. She needed to see Sam. It became her obsession. By the fifth day, her obsession paid off, Sam was hurrying, distracted, towards her. He had his head down and looked deep in thought. Joanna worried that if she didn't say something, she would remain unnoticed and he would walk right past her.

'Hello, Sam,' she was almost blocking his path so that he had no choice but to stop, look up and acknowledge her.

'Joanna! It's good to see that you're out of the hospital. How are you feeling?'

She thought he looked slightly embarrassed to see her but she couldn't let him get away. She had to make things right again between them. 'I'm feeling much better, thank you.' She headed towards a bench, 'Here, have a seat. I'm sure we have a lot of catching up to do.'

'No, I'm sorry, I'm already late for a faculty meeting. Perhaps some other time?'

Joanna sensed that he was squirming. Reluctantly, she knew she had to let him go. 'Sure, it was good bumping into you.'

'You too. Take care.'

Joanna watched Sam almost run away, carrying her crumpled hopes and dreams with him.

When she arrived home, Mark was standing on the doorstep. 'There you are, Joanna. I hope you aren't overdoing things.'

She felt mildly irritated at his concern, but guilty at the same time for feeling that way, 'No, I'm just getting some exercise and fresh air. I need to build up my strength.'

'Let me know next time and I'll join you.'

Joanna ignored this last remark, 'Why are you here?'

If Mark was hurt, he didn't let it show, 'I wanted to check and see if you needed anything.'

'I'm fine, thanks, just need to take a nap.' She certainly didn't feel up to having company.

'Yes, of course. I'll be on my way then. Let me know if I can be of any help.'

Joanna practically closed the door in Mark's face. Why couldn't Sam be the one showing up on her doorstep full of concern? She found herself remembering the last time Mark had called and how they had laughed about Mrs. Bell Bottoms. Was she being too harsh? No, she knew that given the choice, she would always choose to spend her time with Sam, but was it too late? Had her Riverboat Disco already set sail into uncharted waters?

When Mark arrived home, Eloise wasted no time in saying what was on her mind, 'You really shouldn't be getting her hopes up.' Mark looked puzzled, so she elaborated, 'Joanna. She'll start to think that you still have feelings for her and perhaps look at getting back together.'

'I'm just helping out while she recovers. She almost died.'

'You're a Saint, after the way she treated you.'

'We were married for over twenty years, we share a daughter. I can't just switch off my emotions. A part of me will always care.'

'Well don't blame me if she starts calling you every time she needs something.'

Mark had never seen, nor did he like, this side of Eloise. 'To be honest, it wouldn't bother me if she did.' He began to smile as he remembered the conversation about Mrs. Bell Bottoms and shared the anecdote with Eloise. It was obvious that she didn't find it funny.

'I can't believe you both honestly thought that was her name.' Eloise was almost scowling. She had never looked more unattractive.

'I guess you and I don't share the same sense of humour.'

'You call that humour?'

What had gotten into her, or had he just never noticed before?

The headaches were becoming more infrequent and less severe. Soon Joanna felt well enough to go back to work. She booked an appointment to have her hair done for the Saturday beforehand.

Her stylist, Sue, was her usual chatty self, 'Did you enjoy your holiday?'

'Oh, I haven't been on holiday, I was in hospital.' Joanna immediately regretted mentioning the hospital because Sue was the kind of person who would ask a lot of questions.

Instead, she said, 'Did you have to cancel going away then? If so, I hope you got your money back.'

'I was never going away.'

'No? I'm sure that's what you told me last time you were here. I thought you said you were leaving later that day.'

Joanna might have dismissed this as a misunderstanding, especially with the sound of a hairdryer making it hard to hear, except for the fact that she had received a get well card from work and Julie from Accounts had written that she was sorry Joanna hadn't been able to go on her hols. One misunderstanding was permissible, but two? Joanna questioned whether she had indeed had something planned and she hoped it hadn't included Sam. But no, surely he would have said something by now?

All these questions were making her feel uneasy, but she felt like a new person with her hair done, so to celebrate her life gradually returning to normal, she decided to visit her favourite cafe. She sat at a corner table by the window and reflected on how fortunate she was. Even though she had been fighting a headache all day, she still went ahead and ordered a cappuccino. The hot and frothy drink tasted as good as she remembered. It also proved therapeutic. With each sip, she felt the pounding throb in her head slowly subside, until the result was one of absolute clarity. It was then that she remembered. It all came back. The events that had led to the fateful night of the wearing of the pink dress. She remembered methodically planning how it would end. It was important that Sam remembered her as vibrant and dancing. She scheduled some vacation days from work, so as not to arouse suspicion and be discovered too soon. She made several trips to the chemist to buy Paracetamol, but recalled that on the night in question, she also added some other pills she already had in her bathroom cabinet, just to be sure. They turned her Prosecco a vibrant blue. It was quite the enticing cocktail. She looked good when she facetimed with Sam. Their favourite songs played and she laughed and danced, wearing the dress, as though she didn't have a care in the world. But she did. She couldn't go on; she didn't want to live anymore because she couldn't live with herself. Each day and night she was tormented by embarrassment and guilt. Embarrassment at how she had foolishly and selfishly believed she could have a future with Sam, and guilt at the hurt she had caused Abigail, Mark and Mickey. How carelessly she had walked away from her own marriage and then almost broken up Sam's relationship. She was a terrible human being and the world would be better off without her. But she had also failed in her attempt to end it all. Before she lost consciousness, she had felt like she was going to throw up. In her hurry to get to the bathroom, she knocked against the wall in the hallway and the wooden plaque fell and hit her on the head. The shock seemed to abate the nausea and she managed to make it upstairs to bed where she eventually passed out. Poor Abigail had been left to pick up the pieces of her mother's reckless mess, and then she remembered the most important piece of the puzzle - her suicide note. She had written Abigail a letter to say "goodbye" and mailed it. Where was it now? Had Abigail read it? She almost knocked the table over in her haste to leave the cafe and reach her daughter to explain and apologise. It was raining, but she didn't notice. She stood impatiently, waiting for a pause in the traffic so she could cross the road and get to her car. She felt her phone vibrate inside her jacket pocket. As she reached in to answer it, something fell to the ground. Her treasured swan button lay glistening by her foot. She bent down to retrieve it. There was a screeching of brakes, people shouting and a loud thud as she lost her balance, teetered into the road and hit the ground as an oncoming car tried to unsuccessfully swerve and avoid hitting her. The rain felt cold, seeping through her clothes, as all life began to seep out and wash away. Lying on her side, she strained to keep her eyes open as they followed the back of a familiar figure with Marc Bolan curls hurry along the street and disappear from view. The effort proved too much, Joanna closed her eyes for the final time and then she, too, was gone.

Sam and Mickey were getting into party mode. It was a pity it was raining, but the forecast said it would clear up in time for the evening and their going away/engagement party on the river. Giana had flown over especially for the occasion. Mickey had just got back from the newsagents, excitedly holding ten copies of the Italian magazine that featured them both, when she made a dramatic entrance into their living room wearing one of Mickey's designs. It was a mini dress made up of silver mirrors. She wore it with her signature biker boots; this time they were pink sequined and tied with satin ribbon for laces. Mickey was full of admiration.

Soon it was party time and all three piled into a taxi and headed for the pier.

Sam was getting anxious. The journey was taking far longer than usual. 'I hope we aren't going to be late to our own party.'

They had come to a complete halt. The taxi driver turned the cab around, 'We're being diverted. There's an accident up ahead. It's always the bloody same, people just don't know how to drive when it's raining.'

Abigail was spending the rainy, late afternoon sorting through the last of her mail that had accumulated while her mother had been in the hospital. The bills and genuine correspondence had already been taken care of, but she methodically opened what she believed to be advertisements so as not to miss anything important. In order to make the task less laborious, she watched a beloved movie of hers and Joanna's from 1940, Waterloo Bridge. They had watched it so many times, she knew it by heart. Set in London, during WW11, Robert Taylor plays an Officer who falls in love with a ballet dancer played by Vivien Leigh. Abigail had just reached the final scene where Robert Taylor, clutching the now dead Vivien Leigh's lucky charm, recalls her telling him that she would never love anyone else, when an envelope in her mother's handwriting fell out of a circular. She attempted to read the postmark, but it had smudged and was illegible. She paused the movie, and hurriedly read the contents:

My Darling Abigail,

By the time you read this letter I will be gone. I will have left this earth, to remain a loving memory, hopefully one that is always evoked by music. I know this will come as a shock, and the hardest part for me is the realisation of knowing how you will feel as you read these words, and my not being there to comfort you. Please know that my decision, and it is mine alone, has nothing to do with you. No mother could have had a better daughter. The best way to explain my actions is to say that not only can I no longer live in this world with others, I can no longer live with myself; I am haunted and tormented by what I shall refer to only as my 'embarrassments'.

Learn from me, my darling, and not just from my mistakes. I did many things spectacularly right, you are living proof of that. In the words of Marc Bolan, 'Life's a Gas'. It is too late for me, but it is what I wish for you.

Your loving mother, always.

Abigail's only thought was to try and reach her mother in time. Where would she have planned to end it all? At home, on a bridge, the river? Instinctively, she called Joanna's cell phone, hoping against hope that she wouldn't be too late. She willed her mother to answer, afford her the opportunity to talk her out of it, convince her that she still had so much to live for. The call went to voicemail.

'Mum, if you get this message, don't do it and please wait for me. Let me know where you are and we can talk this through. I don't know what I would do without you. I love you so much.'

Abigail ran to her car and headed towards her mother's house. Of course, of all the times, traffic was at a standstill. There was a detour and a Policeman was redirecting them away from the main road.

'What's happened?' Abigail asked him.

'A pedestrian's been hit,' he replied.

She wasn't surprised, no-one knew how to drive in the rain. She made a mental note to be extra careful, even though time was of the essence.

When she reached Coolgardie Avenue, Joanna's car was nowhere to be seen and her house was in darkness, but Abigail had to make sure. She ran into every room frantically calling her mother's name. Nothing was out of place, except for her mother. Where would she have gone? She got back in her car and drove down to the pier. She saw the lights of a boat and she could hear the Bee Gees singing "Stayin' Alive" as another Riverboat Disco prepared to set sail. She ran along the edge of the river calling for Joanna. She continued running onto the bridge. The water appeared dark and murky below, reminding her of her mother's state of mind. 'Please don't be down there,' she half prayed and half whispered, emotion, coupled with the cold, causing her to feel as though she, too, was running out of breath as well as time. The Riverboat Disco passed under the bridge. The song had changed to "Tragedy" and she fell to her knees sobbing. She had left in such haste that she hadn't put on a jacket and she realised she was shivering. It was hopeless. She felt it in her bones, and it wasn't just the cold, she knew she was too late. She made her way back to her car and did what she should have done in the first place, she called the police.

She had only just got home when she heard a knock at the door and there, as she had already anticipated, stood two Police Officers.

112

Abigail spoke first, 'You must be here about my mother,' and she handed them the letter.

They seemed to take forever to read it, but finally one of them said, 'Please accept our condolences.' He handed her back the now already wet with tears piece of paper. 'We will need a copy of this letter to close the accident investigation, and you will need to formally identify the body.'

All Abigail heard was accident. 'Accident? How did she do it?'

The Police Officer who spoke looked awkward. 'Perhaps it would be better if we continue this conversation inside?'

'Oh yes, of course.' Abigail led them into the lounge, Robert Taylor's anguished face stared back at them from the screen, almost accusatory for denying him the chance to conclude his stellar performance.

The Policeman was kind, but still awkward, 'There is no easy way to say this. Your mother fell in front of a car. It was instantaneous. She didn't suffer.'

'Just like Vivien Leigh.'

'Excuse me?'

'It's an old movie I was watching. Vivien Leigh commits suicide by walking in front of traffic on Waterloo Bridge.'

This time both Officers looked awkward, and not knowing how to take their leave, they sat in silence, with the final frame of Waterloo Bridge frozen in time.

CHAPTER SEVENTEEN

It was most out of character, but Rosemary Elphick not only had a change of heart but also a change of plan. She had decided to make her home in Naples, and as she waited for her connecting flight, she flicked through a fashion magazine. Looking up at her from the page was the face of her son. She read that he was premiering his own fashion label, "The House of Harman", in Milan in just a few days. A cornucopia of conflicting emotions took hold, and as she grappled to take control, she also changed her ticket and boarded a flight for Milan.

The new office and showroom for The House of Harman was easy to find. Fortunately for Rosemary, there was a coffee shop right across the street that afforded her an unobstructed view. For three consecutive afternoons, while enjoying a cappuccino, she observed the eclectic and sometimes entertaining mix of people entering and leaving the building. It was easy to spot Mickey. He always stood out from the crowd, but in a good and charismatic way. Each afternoon, around 3:00 pm, he would exit the building and hurry down the street, always alone and turning heads as he went. On the fourth afternoon, Rosemary made her move. Just before 3:00 pm, she left the coffee shop, crossed the street and waited outside The House of Harman. She didn't have to wait long. There was no time for hesitation and she seized the moment.

'Mickey?' Rosemary immediately recognised her son as he danced down the steps of the ornate fronted building that was now home to his collection of designs.

She expected him to not know who she was, but his delay in answering was due to feeling unsure of how to address her. She looked just as he'd imagined from her website photo, perhaps less austere. He settled for 'Hello, Rosemary,' it was too soon to call her mum.

His acknowledgement took her by surprise, 'I know this must be something of a shock, but is there somewhere we can go to talk?'

Yes, it was a shock, initially, but the feeling soon tempered to one of pleasant surprise. 'Yes, of course, there's a nice little coffee place just around the corner.'

Mickey took Rosemary's arm protectively, just like any good son would do, and steered her across the busy street.

Once settled at a table, and with cappuccinos ordered, Rosemary was the first to speak, 'I know you must have a million questions for me.'

Mickey had prepared more than a million questions, in case this day should finally arrive, but now they didn't seem as important and he found himself at a complete loss for words. Instead, he said, 'It is enough that you are here.'

A tear rolled down Rosemary's cheek, 'Oh Mickey, not a day has gone by that I haven't thought about you. I have followed your career and I am so proud of you.'

'I do have one question. Why did you go and see Joanna, and not me?'

'I wanted to find a way to help you, but I wasn't sure if you would want to see me. I hoped that you would find out from Joanna and come and find me, but you didn't.'

'I did come to see you. I drove past your office, but something stopped me from coming in. It didn't feel like the right time.'

'Does this feel like the right time?' So, he had tried to find her, had almost been at her door. She was overcome by an enormous sense of relief.

'Yes, it does.' Mickey wanted to tell her about Sam, and invite her to their wedding, but he decided it should wait, 'Thank you for talking sense into Joanna.'

'I knew she'd come around to my way of thinking and do the right thing. You can always count on me to do whatever it takes to remove any obstacles that stand between my son and the happiness and success he so rightly deserves.' As if to emphasise the fact, she very deliberately took her hand and brushed a wayward curl of hair away from her eyes. It made her appear even more determined, 'It's so sad that she met such a tragic end.'

'How do you know about Joanna's death?'

Rosemary thought fast and replied dismissively, 'It was in one of the local papers. Just a few lines.'

Mickey was relieved that she was his mother; he sensed that Rosemary Elphick was not someone you would ever want to cross. Sam was going to have a formidable mother-in-law.

CHAPTER EIGHTEEN

'Now this one does look interesting. Definitely not something you come across every day.' Audrey reached deeper into the bag of donations and pulled out a screwed up pink ball of sequins and feathers.

Gayle walked over for a closer look. 'My cat would have a field day with that. Just look at all those feathers.'

Audrey gave the dress a good shake and held it up so they could both get a closer look, 'Do you want it?'

'Oh no, I couldn't. It's too good to be used as a cat toy, and I can't see myself wearing it, although perhaps in my younger days. Does it have a label?'

'Yes, look, it says Mickey Harman.'

'Ooh, he's a famous designer from these parts. I wonder who left it? What else is in that bag?'

The two women eagerly emptied the contents onto the counter only to be disappointed. Nothing else came close, just the usual assortment of outdated high street clothes that people were only too happy to offload and donate to their cat rescue charity shop.

'I have an idea. Why don't we raffle this dress? I'm sure we'd be able to sell a lot of tickets.'

'I think that's a brilliant idea,' Gayle replied. 'It could be part of our grand reopening event now that the refurbishment is complete. I'm still worried that having been closed for repairs these past few weeks is going to impact future sales.'

'I wouldn't worry. It doesn't seem to have put people off leaving stuff. We have a mountain of bags to still go through.'

117

They were interrupted by someone knocking on the door. A young woman's face was peering through the glass and pointing at the dress.

Audrey pulled a face, 'Oh dear, I do hope that isn't the owner of the dress having a change of heart.' She gave a heavy sigh, 'We'd better see what she wants.' Audrey reluctantly unlocked the door.

Without waiting to be invited, the young woman eagerly stepped inside, 'I hope you don't mind; I know you don't open until 10, but I was on my way to work and happened to notice that exquisite pink dress. I'd like to buy it.' She pulled out her purse, 'How much is it?'

Gayle stepped forward, 'It's not for sale. We're going to raffle it.'

For a moment the young woman appeared crestfallen, but then her face brightened, 'Tell you what, let me buy it now, I'll only wear it the once and then I'll give it back to you to raffle.'

Audrey didn't even stop to consider the offer, 'No, I'm sorry, is there something else in the shop that you......'

Undeterred, the young woman continued, 'I'll take really good care of it and I promise I'll get it cleaned afterwards. I'll even buy a dozen raffle tickets to show my gratitude.'

Audrey was also undeterred, 'Why does it have to be this dress? I'm sure there are others. I have to ask, what's the occasion?'

The woman hesitated, choosing her words carefully, 'It's a bittersweet event, a celebration of someone's life. There'll be lots of music, Kylie, Abba, Disco, and this dress is perfect. I'll never find another that comes close to honouring her memory.'

This time it was Gayle who spoke, 'Well, put like that, how can we say 'no'?'

Audrey nodded her approval.

'Oh thank you. I promise I'll take good care of it so you're able to make a ton of money from your raffle. Wouldn't it be funny if I won it?'

Audrey was already writing up a receipt.

Gayle popped the dress in a bag, 'There you go. Wear it in joy and wear it in love.'

'Thank you so much. You won't regret this.' The young woman practically danced out of the shop.

Audrey walked over to the remaining pile of clothes still sitting on the counter, 'Well that was an unusual and eventful start to the day.'

Gayle agreed, and both women went back to sorting out the more mundane paraphernalia that had been left in their charge.

Julie left the shop and hurried on to work. It didn't matter that she would get dirty looks from the rest of accounting for being late, finding this dress made up for everything. It was the perfect way to bid farewell to her co-worker. She knew Joanna would approve.

This really was the party to end all parties; a musical celebration of Joanna's life. Abigail had chosen to hold the gathering at her mother's house. The mantel was adorned with photos of Joanna throughout the years, many with her wearing a shirt adorned with the name of a band. Abigail had hung the plaque that read, "I may be old, but that's ok, I got to see Marc Bolan in concert!", above the mantel and below, holding centre stage, was a photo taken of a very young Joanna, standing outside the venue in 1977, wearing her "Dandy in the Underworld'" tour t shirt. Abigail had also replaced the centre light with a disco ball. The guests, like the music, were an eclectic mix. Neighbours, old friends, parents of Abigail's school friends, co-workers, the many people Joanna had touched along the way and, of course, Mark and Sam. Mickey was the only one absent. Sam apologised on his behalf, explaining that he was already back in Italy preparing for his inaugural fashion show in Milan.

With every song, someone had a recollection and anecdote of where they had been with Joanna when they first heard it. Disco, Motown, Glam Rock, the songs of Eurovision, the list was endless but none appeared out of place; all evoked fond memories of Joanna. Julie from Accounts entertained them all with her memory of the office holiday party which had been a fancy dress affair. Joanna had arrived dressed as Marc Bolan, complete with a curly wig, glitter under her eyes and wearing a satin jacket, satin trousers and a pink feather boa. With a tennis racket for a guitar, she had asked the DJ to play "20th Century Boy" and had proceeded to impersonate Marc and bop around the dance floor.

'Where'd you get that dress, Julie? It's perfect for this evening,' asked one of the guests.

'Isn't it great and I know Joanna would approve. Would you believe I found it in a charity shop only a couple of days ago?'

She gave everyone a twirl. The light from the disco ball illuminated the sequins and the feathers danced in the breeze.

'It looks exactly like something Kylie would wear. Pink's your colour.'

Abigail was intrigued, 'Did I hear you say you got it from a charity shop?'

'Yes, the cat and kitten one in the High Street.'

All Abigail could think was how mortified Mickey would be if he ever found out. Even in death, Joanna was making sure she still had the final say. While Julie thought she was the cat's meow, if Abigail had been able to see the expression on her mother's face, she was sure she would have looked like the cat who got the cream.

Sam excused himself from the gathering to answer his phone. It was Mickey.

'Hi, sorry to call in the middle of this, but I thought I should say a few words to Abigail.'

Sam was pleasantly surprised at this apparent change of heart. 'Of course, I'll get her for you.'

'How is she holding up?'

'Surprisingly well, but it is a lovely tribute, a true celebration of Joanna. You'd love the music.' Sam chose not to disclose that the pink dress was also in attendance.

'I'm sorry I can't be there. Did you make my excuses?'

'Yes, I did. It was understood. I'll get Abigail.' Sam walked back into the room and over to the mantel where Abigail was standing alone looking at her mother's photo. 'Abigail, Mickey would like to speak to you.' Sam handed her the phone.

'Hello, Mickey. I hear you're making a real name for yourself in Italy.'

Mickey thought she sounded rather awkward but refused to lose his resolve. He jumped right in, 'Abigail, I never got the chance to say how sorry I am about your mother. I know we never really got along, but Joanna was a good friend to Sam and she had excellent taste in music. Please believe me when I say that I will miss her.'

'Thank you, Mickey, hearing that from you means a lot. I know we've had our differences but please let's try and put the difficulties of the past behind us. I know that's what my mum would have wanted.' It took every ounce of restraint but she, too, decided not to mention the dress which was gyrating in all its glory just a few feet away from her.

'Perhaps you'll consider visiting us in Rome sometime?'

'Yes, I'd love that. Thank you.'

With the conversation now bordering on pleasantries, Mickey decided it was time to end the call, 'Take care of yourself and I hope to see you soon. Would you mind handing me back to Sam?'

'Of course. Look after yourself.' Abigail found Sam standing in the hallway. She handed him back his phone and went back to join the guests.

'Everything okay?' Sam asked Mickey.

'Yes, but I have some news for you. Rosemary got in touch with me. I found her waiting for me outside the fashion house.'

'That is a surprise. How did it go?'

'Surprisingly well. We cleared the air. I was rather shocked that she knew what happened to Joanna. She said it was in the local paper.'

'I never saw anything.'

'No? Well, she did say it was only a couple of lines.'

'I miss you, Mickey.'

'I miss you too, but you'll soon be here. We have a very important wedding to attend.'

'That's an understatement if ever I heard one. I can't wait.'

'Me neither. Love you.'

'Love you more.' Sam put his phone in his pocket and went back into the room. He suddenly felt very lonely in the crowd.

The music continued. Alcazar "Crying at the Discotheque"' was followed by Phil Collins "One More Night".

'Your mum only tolerated this song because of me.'

Abigail gave her dad a reassuring hug. 'You're wrong, dad. Mum appreciated all genres of music and I know this song held a special place in her heart because of you.'

'I used to refer to the songs she liked as galloping horse music. I wish I had been more considerate of her feelings. I never stopped loving her. There never was anything lasting between Eloise and me. I wanted her to think there was because I was so hurt. I was prepared to give our marriage another try.'

Abigail was taken aback by his confession. She thought long and hard before she spoke, 'Mum had lost the art of being happy. Only music could lift her spirit and she believed it held the key. She wouldn't accept that happiness has to first come from within. I don't know if she was prepared, or wanted, to search deep enough inside herself to find out and now we'll never know.'

She felt the tears she had tried so hard to hold back throughout the evening begin to sting her eyes. As if in answer, and right on cue, Marc Bolan began to sing "Life's a Gas". Sam was suddenly there next to her. All three held hands and joined in the chorus.

Abigail was sure that Joanna and Marc Bolan were singing along with them in Heaven. She made a promise that from now on she was going to live her life to the full and every day as though it were her last. A life lesson learned from her mum.

A DISCO FOR TWO

It was the wedding to end all weddings. High on a clifftop, with a panoramic view of Capri, Mickey and Sam said their vows. The wedding party were all resplendent in outfits designed by Mickey, created by his own fashion label, "The House of Harman". Mickey wore a white satin suit and a yellow feather boa and Sam wore a grey cotton sateen suit with a yellow tie. Giana vowed that she wanted to eat, sleep and die in her bridesmaid dress, an elaborate but flattering cocktail of lemon tulle and grey satin ribbon.

Mickey had also designed his mother's outfit. Rosemary was resplendent in a royal blue silk jersey dress that draped her petite frame beautifully. She couldn't remember the last time she had got so dressed up, nor felt so glamourous and sophisticated. The dress would forever remind her of this exceptional and special day. Mickey had requested that both Rosemary and his adoptive mother walk him up the aisle. The two most important women in his life stood either side of him, linked his arms, and the trio walked along the grass path, between the seated guests, to where Sam was waiting. Rosemary would always define this moment as the one of which she was most proud. The whole world knew she was Mickey's mother. Giana walked behind them singing the song "Wedding Bell Blues", but changing the name in the lyrics from Bill to Sam. As she sang, 'Come on and marry me Sam', all the guests cheered, clapped and joined in the chorus. It took a while for the exuberant crowd to quieten down, but when they did, Sam and Mickey each read their own personally written promises to one another. When the short but moving ceremony was over, Giana sang, "Celebration", as she led everyone to a gigantic marquee for the reception.

Sam sat down next to Rosemary after exhausting himself on the dance floor. 'I'm so pleased that you and Mickey found one another again. I guess we have Joanna to thank for that. I still can't believe she's no longer with us.'

'Yes, such a tragic turn of events.'

'She never struck me as someone who would choose to take her own life.'

The look on Rosemary's face immediately said it all. Embarrassed, Sam apologised, 'Oh, I'm terribly sorry. How inconsiderate of me. Of course, they probably didn't put that in the paper, to protect the family. She wrote poor Abigail a note.'

'It's alright. You weren't to know, but it has come as a shock.' It was an entirely different shock to the one Sam imagined. Rosemary could not believe her luck.

It was the murder to end all murders and Rosemary had committed it. It wasn't only bad people who did bad things; good people, with the right motivation and poor judgement, also did bad things. This mantra had always been her first line of reasoning when defending clients. Now she was defending herself, with her conscience the harshest jury she had ever faced. She thought back to that rainy afternoon. She certainly hadn't planned to commit murder, but then she hadn't expected to see Joanna, nor been prepared to be overwhelmed by the feelings of anger and resentment that the very sight of her had evoked. She used the same rationale as if it had been a crime of passion.

'I know, I know, but there's no need to give me such an accusatory look.' Her late husband stared back at her. She picked up the photo, caressed his face with her finger and felt his disappointment. She was sure it was the first time he had ever disapproved of something she had done; they hadn't always agreed, nor seen eye to eye, but he had always understood. Until now. But then she had never killed someone before and, worse still, deliberately. There was a first time for everything. 'I'm sorry. Joanna meant to end it all anyway. I just gave her a helping hand and moved things along. Why, she might have intended to step in front of the car at the same time as I pushed her. Perhaps she was already stepping out into the road and I'm not to blame at all. Now, there's a thought, almost a happy coincidence?'

Try as she might, she knew there was no convincing him, or herself. She had done a terrible and unforgivable thing and, what made it worse, was that she had got away with it. There would be no accountability. And what about Mickey? He had a murderer for a mother. At least he still had a mother, two now, if you included the one who had adopted him. But Abigail had lost the only mother she ever had. Abigail had none. Rosemary wondered how she was coping. She began to cry; big, racking sobs. She had to find a way to make amends. She couldn't bring Joanna back, but she could do something nice for Abigail to make her life a little easier. After all, that's what mothers did. She would provide her with a golden opportunity. She dried her eyes, composed herself, picked up the phone and called Stephen Thompson, Managing Partner at Thompson, Rodgers and Ruhle, a prestigious law firm in the City. Rosemary and her late husband had been active in their mentoring programme for aspiring law students.

'Hello Stephen. This is Rosemary Elphick.'

'Rosemary, how wonderful to hear your voice. I'm not one for gossip but rumour has it you've shut up shop and moved to Italy. Can I coax you back? I have a case that I think would both intrigue and challenge you.'

'Thank you, Stephen, but no, I'm not even tempted. I'm very happy with my new life here in Naples. However, I do know of a young paralegal who would be quite the asset to your firm.'

'High recommendation, indeed. Please tell me more.'

'Her name is Abigail Stevens. I am asking you to assign her a place on the Junior Associate Programme.'

There was silence at the other end while he waited for her to elaborate. She was not forthcoming. 'Are those the only details you're providing me?'

'Stephen, you don't need to know anymore, you have my word. I'll email you her contact information. You won't regret it.'

'You always were a formidable adversary and a hard person to refuse, my dear Rosemary, both in and out of the courtroom. I'll get the offer letter out to her once you've sent me her address.'

'Thank you, Stephen. You won't regret it. Oh, and one last but very important request, please don't mention to Abigail that it was me who put her name forward. It is of the utmost importance that I remain anonymous.'

'You also were, and continue to be, an intriguing woman. I'll respect your wishes. Abigail won't hear it from me.'

'And please let me know, periodically, how she's getting along.'

'I'll be happy to.'

'Thank you. Let me know if you ever fancy a holiday in Naples. I run a great bed and breakfast and I'll be happy to show you around.'

'You can count on it. Take care, it was good hearing from you.'

'There, I'm convinced I've done the right thing. I've taken the first step towards making amends. Don't you agree? I feel much better for it.' She held the photo again. It was one of her favourites, taken on a cruise. He looked relaxed and happy. His hair was windswept by the ocean breeze and you could sense that the sun felt warm on his face. She kissed it. His lips were cold.

Abigail hesitated before opening the envelope. It wasn't every day that she got a letter sent to her home address from the rock stars of the legal world, Thompson, Rodgers and Ruhle. It could only mean one of two things: it had been mistakenly sent to her home instead of work, or she was in deep trouble. It was neither.

Dear Ms. Stevens,

We take great pleasure in writing to offer you a place at our firm within our highly commended Rising Star Associate & Scholarship Program. As you may already be aware, this program was founded by our Managing Partner, Stephen Thompson, more than ten years ago, to enable young people to pursue a law degree, while gaining valuable insight and work experience as employees of our firm, mentored by our established attorneys.

You come highly recommended to us and we would welcome the opportunity to meet with you. Please contact me at the number above to schedule an appointment for an introductory meeting.

We know that you will be a valuable member of our team and look forward to continuing our association in person.
Sincerely,
Melissa Symon
New Intake Coordinator, RSASP

Abigail didn't waste a moment. She couldn't wait to share her news. She called Tim.

After her mother's death, Abigail took up running. She planned to outrun her grief. She ran every day, and every day she ran a little further. On weekends, she ran further still and, on this particular Sunday, found herself having to stop to catch her breath outside an animal sanctuary. A donkey ambled over and nudged her arm. 'I'm sorry, but I don't have any carrots or apples for you. If, in fact, that's what you're hoping for.' She noticed a rather attractive young man watching her. She felt self-conscious and quickly carried on talking to the donkey, 'I know horses like apples, but I'm not entirely sure about donkeys.' As if not believing her, the donkey nudged her again. 'I think he wants to be friends,' she continued, eventually finding the confidence to acknowledge the attractive man.

'The donkey's not the only one,' he walked over, 'Hi, I'm Tim.'

'Nice to meet you, Tim. I'm Abigail. Do you work here?'

'I volunteer on the weekends. I'm training to be a veterinarian at the local college. In my final year.'

'You must really love animals.'

'I do. And you?'

'Oh yes, I love animals, too.'

He smiled a warm, genuine smile, 'No, I was asking what you do for a living.'

'Oh, silly me,' Abigail found herself blushing, 'I'm a paralegal at a local law firm.'

'You probably run to relieve the stress?'

'Not from work. I recently lost my mum and it's an outlet for my grief.'

'I'm so sorry.'

'She took her own life.' Abigail couldn't believe she had blurted it out to a complete stranger. What had come over her? 'I do apologise.'

'What for?'

'You didn't need to know that.'

'It sounds like you could use a friend. My shift's about over. Would you like to get something to eat? There's a new vegetarian place just opened," Beets and Pulses". Do you fancy giving it a try?'

'Yes, please. I've just realised I'm feeling quite hungry. Are you a vegetarian?'

'I try to be. Most of my charges here were rescued from slaughter. I wouldn't be able to hold my head high and look them in the eye otherwise. Just give me a moment to clean up and get my stuff. I'll be right back.'

While Abigail waited for Tim to return, she reflected that the next place she wanted to run was straight into his arms. She wondered if this was how Joanna felt when she first set eyes on Sam and regretted judging her so harshly. She hadn't believed in love at first sight………until now.

Abigail was relieved to find that "Beets and Pulses" was busy. She didn't want to draw attention to herself as she was sure she looked like a lovesick teenager. She hoped she would get lost in the crowd. As Abigail coyly pretended to study the menu, Tim unabashedly focused all of his attention on her.

'So, have you ever wanted to be a lawyer?'

'I had thought about it, which is why I became a paralegal. I wanted to test the waters working in the legal field before I committed to the years involved and the expense of studying for a law degree. But since I lost my mum, I think I might just go for it. I would like to put it to good use and help the vulnerable. Maybe specialise in family law, help out at a legal clinic.'

The waitress came to take their order. Tim sensed, correctly, that Abigail was emotional from talking about her mother, and ordered for her. After the waitress had left, and Abigail had composed herself, Tim continued the conversation. He sensed that even though it was upsetting, Abigail needed, and would welcome, the opportunity to talk more about Joanna's death.

He gently coaxed her, 'I know your mum would be very proud of you.'

'I hope so. I can't get rid of this feeling that I let her down. I should have seen the signs. I knew she was upset. She was getting divorced from my dad and had already fallen hard for someone, but it didn't work out. I knew she was hurting. I just didn't realise how badly. The worst of it is that I knew the relationship was doomed, practically from the start. I was becoming quite exasperated with her. Perhaps, if I had been kinder and more patient, she would have opened up a lot more to me.'

'If she was that determined, and it sounds as though she was, I don't think anything you could have done or said would have changed the eventual outcome.'

Their food arrived and Abigail realised that this was the first time she had looked forward to a meal since the suicide, 'This looks delicious. I'm ravenous.'

'Good to hear. You need to keep up your strength, especially with all the exercise you're getting.'

'I get the sense you're a very caring person, Tim. I guess you'd have to be to do the job you do.'

'I must admit to having a soft spot for paralegals who have recently lost their mum.'

'Have you known many?'

'No, you're the first.' He gave her a look that made her melt.

From that moment on, they were inseparable.

When she told Tim about the letter, he was as excited as her. 'I'd like to come with you to the interview. We could make a day of it.'

'I'd love that. I'll let you know the date. I still can't believe it. It's a dream come true.'

'You deserve this and so much more. I love you.'

'Love you too. I'm going to call them now.'

Thompson, Rodgers and Ruhle occupied a very modern building in the heart of the city. Tim went to wait for her in a cafe, conveniently located next door. Abigail took the elevator to the 10th floor and gave her name to the receptionist. She noticed a beautiful and colourful glass sculpture and wondered if it was a Chihuly. When she saw that it was nailed to the table, she was convinced. She didn't have to wait long before Melissa, the New Intake Coordinator, introduced herself and ushered them both into an equally impressive conference room. There was so much glass, it was hard to instantly recognise what was open space. Abigail wondered how many people had been sent to the hospital with concussion. As if reading her thoughts, Melissa explained that they had only recently moved into the premises and some were finding it difficult to get used to the openness of it all. Abigail said she felt very comfortable and that it didn't worry her at all. Melissa talked a little about the history of the firm and then described the Rising Star Programme in detail. When she had finished, Abigail was aware of a tall and distinguished man standing in the doorway. She was sure she recognised him from a TV current affairs show as someone who provided insightful commentary. He introduced himself as Stephen Thompson. Melissa sat in for a few minutes and then left.

'So, Abigail, you come highly recommended and we are thrilled to have you on board, but what do you hope to bring to the table?' Stephen Thompson casually relaxed back in his chair, all the time wondering what was Abigail's connection to Rosemary.

Abigail thought carefully before replying, 'I want to be able to use my expertise to help the disadvantaged and I know that you encourage staff to donate many hours to Pro Bono work and legal clinics.'

Ah, so that was it. Rosemary always was a champion of the underdog. That's how their paths must have crossed.

'I'm glad to hear it. You will have ample opportunity to do just that. I'm sure you will be a great addition to the team. Prior to starting with us, you will have the chance to meet the others in the Programme at a weekend retreat. Melissa will send you the details.' He got up to leave.

'When will I know if I've been accepted?' Abigail thought she must have given a terrible impression for the interview to end so abruptly.

'You were already accepted when you received our letter. This meeting was a formality to get us on a more personal footing. Congratulations and welcome to the Firm, Abigail.' He shook her hand.

Abigail had never been handed anything on a plate before, because that's how it felt. She was still having trouble processing it all as she entered the cafe and told Tim.

'I think a celebration is in order.' He had never seen her look more beautiful. 'Let's plan to go to a fancy restaurant one night next week but, right now, let's find you a posh frock to wear.'

Nothing could dampen her enthusiasm, not even when she couldn't find just the right dress. 'Don't worry, I already have a few outfits I can jazz up. My mum taught me one or two things about accessorising.'

EPILOGUE

And now, the evening had arrived and they were going out to celebrate. Tim arrived before she was ready. He was holding a box, tied with a big red bow.

'This is for you to wear tonight. I must be truthful. I won it in a raffle. I didn't even know what the prizes were, but I wanted to support the charity. They rescue cats and kittens. Anyway, I think it worked out rather well, for all of us.'

Abigail undid the bow. She removed the lid and there it was again, just like a boomerang, the object of her mother's affections returned to her: the pink sequined dress. At first, Abigail felt lost and confused, but she also felt that her mother was reassuringly by her side. The lyrics to "Life's a Gas" resounded in her head and she knew that it really didn't matter at all.

'Do you like it?' Tim looked concerned as though he had done entirely the wrong thing.

Abigail rushed to reassure him, 'I love it, Tim. It's perfect and I can't wait to wear it for our date tonight. Thank you.'

'One more very important thing. This I didn't win in a raffle. I chose it just for you and I hope you'll say yes.' He slipped an engagement ring on her finger.

'Yes, Yes, YES! You've made me the happiest girl in the world.' Abigail meant every word. Tonight, she would wear the dress in joy and in love. It was Joanna's wish.

THE END

About the Author

Katherine Martino is originally from East London but currently resides on the East Coast of the USA. She has written bios and press releases for a small, Nashville based record label. She has a penchant for puns, the late rock musician Marc Bolan, for whom she worked during the 1970's, and the Eurovision Song Contest.

Printed in Great Britain
by Amazon